Shundra Henderson,

THORNS AND ROSES

Shundra Henderson,

THORNS AND ROSES

ANNETTE WHITAKER-MOSS

Disclaimer

This is a work of fiction. Names, characters, businesses, places, events, locales, and incidents are either the products of the author's imagination or used in a fictitious manner. Any resemblance to actual persons, living or dead, or actual events is purely coincidental.

ISBN 978-0-9897657-2-5

WORDS OF WISDOM

Proverbs 16:3
Commit to the LORD whatever you do, and your plans will succeed.

Proverbs 16:9

In his heart a man plans his course, but the LORD determines his steps.

Rose Bud
Imaginations
The promise of new beginnings

www.annettewhitaker.com

Table of Contents

1

Reminiscing

Imagine walking alone in a park on a beautiful, quiet day where the temperature is 73 degrees, with a slight breeze by the lake. Without a care in the world, your mind is free to roam across the lake as far as the eye can see. In any given direction you can easily focus on a bucket list, or a nice vacation, or even secret memories of the past. For a split second, if Shundra Henderson didn't know any better, she would have thought today was one of those days because of the calmness and peacefulness that surrounded her: an enchanted and well-deserved vacation. Unfortunately, it wasn't. She had just gotten off from work and decided to spend a few moments by the lake to clear her thoughts. It was a hectic day, especially with the company celebrating her seventh year of employment, which was an excellent way of showing their appreciation; but in her job, time is crucial, and she felt overworked and would have preferred a vacation instead. She was daydreaming, feeling somewhat relaxed, and then suddenly, her mind shifted to wishing someone special was in her life to share the moment. She was also dealing with mixed emotions involving how much she loved her job but wanted to move on to something less stressful. She thought, *Wouldn't it be nice to have someone special that appreciated me, a true friend, a future husband to help relieve the stress, and a lover that enjoyed exploring the world and the true meaning of intimacy?*

She began to reminisce over the good old days when she was very young, not knowing a thing about love but having a crush on a boy named Bobby who lived across the street from her. Their relationship was kind of funny, since the two of them were only ten years old, and at that age, what did they know about being a girlfriend or a boyfriend?

If Bobby saw Shundra standing outside, he would ride his bicycle in front of her house and do something silly to get her attention. One day when no one was around, he decided to have a conversation with her. Shundra did not recall what the discussion was about, but she did remember telling him if he didn't leave her alone, she would hit him. You know, *girl likes boy sort of thing!*

Of course, he didn't believe she would hit him, so he dared her to do so. Spontaneously, she picked up a stick that was nearby and popped him right across the forehead. He dropped his bike, grabbed his head, and with a loud shout, he said, "Ouch! Why did you do that? Are you crazy?" He couldn't believe it and neither could she, especially since she liked him. It was a spur-of-the-moment sort of thing that wasn't supposed to happen. Shundra never thought he would dare her to hit him. *Who dares people these days?* she thought. Now, because she said she would, she had to be true to her word.

She wasn't sure if he would ever speak to her again. But, from that day forward, until her family moved out of the neighborhood, the two of them had a boyfriend/girlfriend thing going on. Smiling and giggling at one another was the highlight of their day. Those were the good old days, acting like silly kids without a care in the world.

Shundra was helplessly grinning from ear to ear while thinking, if only life were that simple. She looked at her watch and realized it was getting late. It was still a good time to be sitting by the lake, but she had to get home in time to attend the swing dance class.

Shundra looked forward to dancing on Monday and Wednesday nights. Not only was it good exercise for her, but it also helped to relieve the stress after a hard day of work.

It was Wednesday night, and she had 30 minutes to spare before heading home and preparing for her class. So, she crossed her legs and gazed at the water while smiling as she began to reminisce again about all the schoolboy crushes she'd encountered as a young girl.

She would never forget the encounter with the school bully, Roderick Sinclair, while getting acquainted with her new surroundings and friends.

Roderick must have come from a rough side of town because he didn't know how to show kindness to anyone; and of all the girls at the school, he had a crush on Shundra. Instead of being nice to her, he terrorized her by pinning her against the wall and daring her to move. If she tried to run, he would grab her arm so tight that it left a bruise for several days. The intimidation was too much for a young girl who had never encountered such rudeness. He was about five feet tall—gigantic, in her eyes—and very dreadful-looking. Tears fell from her eyes every time she came face-to-face with him.

Shundra didn't understand the real meaning of sin, but she knew it was when someone did something wrong. That much, she learned in Sunday school. Thinking back, she realized the word "sin" was in Roderick's last name, and that explained everything because there was nothing but wickedness in his behavior. She felt Roderick's last name should be "SIN DECLARED," boldly pronounced and clearly understood by anybody that crossed his path.

He was the terror that harassed her for the whole 4th-grade school year, and every single day that he could.

Shundra had become very good at hiding after school until all the kids left the premises, including Roderick. He was the last one to go, and she had to practically run to get home within the timeframe allowed by her mom. It took 30 minutes to walk home, but her mom allowed her an hour. Anything past an hour meant trouble for Shundra, and heaven forbid if she missed that deadline! Dealing with Roderick was terrible enough, but dealing with her mom would be worse, and she had no desire to face her mom's fury.

Roderick seemed to have disappeared by the time she made it to the 5th grade. Whether he moved or dropped out of school did not matter to her. Finally, she could live and enjoy school like a normal kid without looking over her shoulder. She never saw him again.

It wasn't long before she met Marcus Chapman, who appeared to be kind, funny, and handsome, with a cool-looking afro. He was in the 6th grade, approaching graduation and moving on to Fuller Middle School. Shundra was in the 5th grade with another year before she could move to Fuller.

Stonewall Jackson Elementary School, where she attended, had two buildings. The first building was the main building with the principal's office, cafeteria, library, teachers' lounge, and kindergarten through 5th grade. The second building was for the 6th-graders only. Somehow during recess, Shundra and Marcus's paths crossed and they began to smile and speak to one another occasionally. Nothing developed between the two of them because several months later, Marcus moved on to Fuller.

The remaining days at Stonewall without Marcus present became a long and quiet year. Seeing him at recess was the best part of

4

Shundra's day. Now, she felt like the new kid in the school, lonely and intimidated. Mentally, she felt everyone was staring and probably talking about her. In reality, she was merely in unfamiliar territory, uncomfortable with not knowing anyone, and overwhelmed with the lack of friendliness.

She didn't remember feeling that way in her old neighborhood. *Maybe it is because they all grew up together,* she thought. It seemed like a lifetime, but finally, the day came when she moved on to Fuller Middle School. She couldn't wait to see Marcus, and she was hoping Marcus had not forgotten her.

It was exciting because she was looking forward to new adventures and seeing Marcus again. *Oh, what better way to start the 7th grade as an adolescent; puppy love and smiles!*

Shundra glanced at her watch again and realized it was time to go. She called her friend Gayle, whom she had known since elementary school, and confirmed their plan to meet at the dance class. For the past eight months, the two of them attended swing dance classes twice a week. It started out being something different to do instead of talking on the phone and sitting around the house waiting on miracles to happen, like Mr. Right knocking at their front door. Neither of them were getting younger, and neither of them wanted to live the rest of their lives alone. They decided to find a place where they could mix and mingle with others in their age group.

Shundra's brief conversation with her uncle persuaded her to search the web for dance classes and locations nearby. He'd tried swing dancing, which was unusual because he had never danced a day in his life, and he loved it. Shundra enjoyed dancing and decided to give it a try. She found a class near home but did not want to go alone, so she asked Gayle if she wanted to go as well. It turned out to be a pleasant experience, so they decided to learn how to swing dance.

While walking to her car and talking on the phone, she asked Gayle if she remembered Kevin Ruler. *Of course she remembered him. Who wouldn't? He was short, bow-legged, dark skin, very athletic, and very popular with the girls.* Gayle couldn't imagine why in the world Shundra would be thinking of Kevin Ruler. She responded, "Yes, isn't that the lowdown dirty dog that thought he was God's gift to women?"

"Yes, that's him, Shundra said. I was thinking back on the good old days when we were kids, and as I recalled, he was the first-ever to introduce me to the world of cheaters.

Gayle responded, "Girl, if I were you, I would put that thought in a bottle and throw it as far as I could across the lake, and hope it never reaches dry land ever.

Shundra laughed and said, "Girl, you find humor in anything! That's why we are friends. I love the way you keep me in good spirits. I'll see you in class."

She couldn't help but reflect on what Gayle said. She was right. Why think of someone who had three known girlfriends, at the same school, at the same time? That's a memory she should have forgotten; but as she recalled, it was an experience she would always remember because she was so naive, and one of the three girls tangled up in all the confusion.

The three girls met in gym class. However, Kevin, as Shundra knew him, was also known to some by his nickname "T-Bone," and the football team called him by his last name "Ruler," which was fitting because of his actions on the football field. One could easily see where this was leading, but at the time, the three girls had no idea that each of them would soon become enemies. Monica knew him as "T-Bone" and Cynthia knew him as "Ruler." Because Cynthia attended another school for several classes not offered at her school, she was the easiest to deceive. Nonetheless, Shundra and Monica became Kevin's prey too, and everyone was astonished when his scheme began to unfold.

It all started in gym class when Shundra was showing off the sweetheart ring Kevin had given her. Monica took one look at the ring and immediately asked, "Who was it that gave you this ring?"

Shundra had nothing to hide, so she proudly smiled and said,

"My boyfriend, Kevin." Instantly, she knew something was wrong. She could tell by the look on Monica's face, which wasn't a good sign, because Monica had a reputation of her own, and not many people would go against her.

But apparently, it was too late for Shundra. Monica rudely called her a liar and said it was the ring that T-Bone had given her. Supposedly, the two of them had broken up, and Monica gave the ring back to T-Bone in the heat of an argument. Monica threatened to take care of Shundra after school, and then she stormed out of class to find T-Bone.

Meanwhile, Cynthia did not know Kevin played football. The girls never had that conversation. She tried to console Shundra by saying, "I've always known girls that dated football players usually end up with bad relationships, but he's got some nerve!"

Before she could utter another word, Shundra quickly said, "Well, Kevin plays football too.

"Really, said Cynthia. Ruler plays football too, so describe Kevin.

Shundra proceeded with "he's short, bow-legged, dark skin," and Cynthia completed her description by saying, "He's a quarterback, right?"

There were no pieces to the puzzle left. Both Shundra and

Cynthia knew they were talking about the same guy that Monica called her boyfriend too. *This dude is a player!* The only consolation the two of them had at that moment was Monica had left the building, because neither of them wanted to encounter her loud and terrorizing behavior.

Now, because of all the confusion, they needed time to process such a predicament. The ordeal wasn't so bad for Cynthia because, after her two classes, she went back to the main campus. It was easy for her to avoid both Monica and Ruler. On the other hand, Shundra had to face Monica and Kevin, T-Bone, Ruler, or the name of choice, now that his scheme was exposed.

Shundra knew when school was over she needed to waste no time getting home. She had seen how Monica treated her so-called friends that she no longer liked, and wanted to avoid her as much as possible. She walked as fast as she could, and even ran a few times to get home without any confrontations. She knew Monica and her gangbangers would walk behind her, call her names, and say awful things like, "You better run because we're going to kick your ass when we catch you!"

Fortunately, and rightly so, Kevin felt terrible about getting Shundra involved with Monica and her hellish friends. Therefore, he walked her home as if he was her bodyguard whenever he didn't have football practice. On those days, Shundra knew Kevin wouldn't let Monica fight her, but she often wondered what would happen when he wasn't around.

She didn't have to wonder for long. Her bodyguard had practice four days later, and Shundra had no one to defend her or help her get home without a fight. The name-calling became worse than when she was in school, and Shundra was embarrassed when Monica ran behind her and kicked her in the butt several times. It didn't help that five of

Monica's friends, bullies too, came along with her; and Shundra's so-called fan club urged the fight to begin.

On that particular day, lucky for Shundra, she was close to home. As she approached her driveway, her mom, who was looking out of the window, came outside demanding to know why all the kids were in front of her house. Shundra explained to her mom that Monica wanted to fight her over a ring that Kevin had given her. Her mom asked, "Do you want the ring?

"No, said Shundra.

"Well, what's the problem? her mom asked. Just give her back the ring."

Shundra told her mom that Monica didn't want the ring, it was a matter of principle and the fact that Kevin had given away something that was special to her. Shundra's mom tried to explain to Monica that Shundra shouldn't be responsible for the wrong that Kevin had done. But, Monica wasn't trying to hear or understand any logic whatsoever.

Monica and her friends had no respect for adults, so they began to curse and call Shundra's mom names too. Shundra's mom was so furious that she wanted to beat the crap out of Monica herself. But, she realized she was the adult and told Shundra, "If you don't fight her now, you will always be running from her."

Shundra's mom understood very well what she was telling her daughter to do. She also knew that as long as she was standing out there, it would be one-on-one, a fair fight. Shundra trusted her mom and knew she wouldn't let the others jump in, but she had been afraid of Monica ever since the 5th grade when she saw her take a fingernail file and stab a girl in the face during a fight. Monica and Roderick "SIN DECLARED" were cousins, and terrorizing people was hereditary in that family.

Regardless, there was no such thing as a fair fight in Shundra's eyes as far as Monica was concerned, so she decided not to fight Monica under any circumstances. Besides, her decision was justified because she had self-piercing earrings on, and the process wasn't complete until the following week. All she could envision was Monica grabbing the earrings, pulling so hard, and splitting her earlobes.

Shundra's mom tried to convince her one last time to fight the girl, but Shundra refused. She was thinking the whole time *since her mom wanted her to fight so badly, and the fact that her mom could talk the talk and walk the walk, why don't she fight the girl herself, beat her down and get over it!* Instead, her mom left her standing there, walked towards the street and said something to Monica. Shundra had no idea what she said, but whatever it was, it was enough to cause them to leave; and to Shundra's surprise, they did not follow her after school anymore. However, while on the school premises, Monica continued to give her that look and *if looks could kill,* Shundra thought, *heaven knows where she would be today!*

2

Dance Environment Center

Quickly, Shundra changed her clothes and made it to the dance class ten minutes after seven. She gets in line just in time to hear the instructor say, "Basic steps, she turns, he turns, and stationary reverse." Gayle looked at her, smiled, and shook her head as she pointed toward her watch. Shundra was always late for class; five minutes, ten minutes, or whatever. Gayle couldn't remember once when she was on time. Shundra knew exactly what Gayle was thinking and sarcastically smiled back as if she didn't care.

It was almost time for the open floor session, which was where beginners, intermediate, and advanced students practice what they learned. It was also known as the time for flirting and getting to know other interested parties. The ladies were searching for single guys just as much as the guys were searching for single women.

Gayle's eyes were on this tall, dark, bold, and handsome-looking guy that seemed to be acquainted with all the instructors. He wasn't shy, and neither was she. When the clock struck 9:00 p.m., prince charming came immediately to Gayle and asked if she wanted to dance. Of course, there was no hesitation on Gayle's part. She was up and ready before he could finish asking the question.

A few good-looking guys came to Shundra for a dance, but she said, "No, not right now." She wanted to relax and enjoy the music. The classes took place at Dance Environment Center, also known as DEC, which had a cozy setup of three dance floors with tables and chairs surrounding them: two small ones, one for the beginners, and the intermediates, and one that was huge for the advanced class and the open floor session.

It was a non-smoking environment that sold snacks, such as chips, water, soda, and sometimes fish and fries, but no liquor. Liquor was allowed, but you must bring it yourself, and most people brought it during the activities sponsored on the weekends and special holidays. However, some brought liquor for the open floor sessions, but not very many.

Shundra and Gayle happened to be sitting at a table with a couple who brought liquor and politely offered to share. Shundra wasn't dancing, so she accepted their kindness and waited as she played hard to get *in her mind* while sipping on the rum and Coke. She was from the old school where guys pursued girls, and she loved the chase.

She wanted to be wined and dined and eventually involved in a committed relationship. She wasn't for the so-called "friends with benefits" stuff where no commitments were required. So, she sat there, observing how the guys conducted themselves.

She presumed which ones would be a good catch if any happen to come her way. Some of them were maybes; a few of them would never look her way; and others, she thought, *No way in this lifetime!*

While observing, she smiled and listened to one of her favorite songs, "On the Ocean," by K' Jon. The melody was soothing, and she loved the lyrics:

Now the tide is coming near (now the tide is coming in)
I see the waves flowing
Out there on the ocean
I know my ship is coming in (and I know my ship is
coming in baby)
Just pass the horizon
(And where) And right where the sky ends
Cause out there on the ocean
I know, I Know, I know, I know, I know, I know, is
coming in
Been waiting too long
But this moment
My ship has finally come

Since it was a weeknight, Gayle and Shundra left DEC around 11:30 p.m. so the two of them could prepare for work in the morning. The rum and Coke made Shundra very relaxed. When she got home and ready for bed, she quickly fell asleep. She began to dream almost immediately. Her mind still fixated on the lyrics and the melody of "On the Ocean," the good old days, and relationships with guys she encountered in her younger days lead back to Marcus.

3

Marcus Chapman

Deeply hidden in her subconscious was Marcus Chapman, for as fate or the inevitable would have it, her dream began precisely one year and two months later, during the second week of Fuller Middle School where she saw him last. Just like the first time she saw him in elementary school, their eyes met, and both of them smiled and kept walking. Shundra was happy to see him, but a little puzzled by his reaction. She thought it would be more like love at first sight, even though it had been a year since they last saw one another. She was beginning to think that maybe he had forgotten her.

Because she was shy and not acquainted with approaching boys, she did not speak up, and things did not change as quickly as she would have liked. She began to wonder if he was ever attracted to her or if maybe he was now attracted to someone else. Feeling disappointed, she decided if that was how it was going to be, then so be it. But miraculously, while she was still in the 8th grade, Marcus decided to say more than hello to her. After all this time, he welcomed her to middle school.

Shundra thought it was funny because the welcoming was a year late; but every day afterward, he would say a little more than before to let her know he was interested. Towards the end of his first year in the 9th grade, Marcus asked Shundra if she walked home or if she rode the school bus home. He was happy to hear that she was walking home. He smiled mischievously, knowing he planned to start walking with her every day. If things had been the way Shundra wanted, Marcus would have been walking her home last year.

Somehow, things began to head in the right direction, and Shundra was very thankful. Though sometimes, she had to walk slower than usual for Marcus to catch up with her, she didn't mind because she was always glad to see him. But, she still had to abide by the house rules, which was to get home within the hour.

She cherished the time that she and Marcus spent together laughing, smiling, and now and then holding hands. She did not want any of those precious moments wasted. She dreaded when she came closer to 6505 Lost Wood Drive because she knew her blissful moments would suddenly end.

Like clockwork, precisely at 3:30 p.m., Shundra's mom would start washing the dishes. More than likely, it was her way of knowing Shundra had not missed her curfew. Shundra and Marcus always walked through a vacant lot between two homes on the next street. It just so happened that the kitchen sink faced the window towards the vacant lot, which made it easy to see when Shundra got closer to home.

Shundra's mom was very proactive. If she did not see Shundra walking across that vacant lot around 3:30 p.m., her speech was already prepared, and from experience, Shundra knew it wasn't anything she wanted to hear.

Shundra made sure Marcus walked at least an arm's length away from her before making that right turn into the vacant lot. That way, her mom had no reason to approach her in front of Marcus and embarrass her if she happened to see any holding hands between the two of them.

Marcus thought it was all foolishness. One day, he decided to voice his opinion and said, "Nothing ever happened from two people holding hands." Shundra's mom agreed, but she knew the possibilities of something more than holding hands could escalate when adolescence was involved. She said holding hands was like an accident waiting to happen, and she wasn't in no position to handle any accidents. She was not compromising; no holding hands were the rule, and that ended the conversation. Of course, Marcus and Shundra decided to let her mom continue to think they were abiding by the rules. *After all, what she didn't know wouldn't hurt her, or them,* they thought.

Eventually, when Shundra was in the 9th grade, her parents allowed her to talk on the phone with Marcus. They were also allowed to meet at the skating rink for parties, and sometimes go to what was called garage parties back in those days. Disco lights and special greetings on the wall with glow-in-the-dark paint was the hip hop thing back then. The music was jamming with some of the greatest hits, like "Flash Light" by Parliament; "Play That Funky Music White Boy" by Wild Cherry; "Brick House" by the Commodores; "Lady's Night" by Kool and the Gang; and now and then they were able to sneak a slow song on, like "Turn off the Lights" by Teddy Pendergrass. But, not without an adult snooping like a private investigator to see what was going on in the dark! They chaperoned the party as they watched to pull the teenagers apart when dancing too close or, if necessary, ask them to leave if they had a problem following the rules.

Of course, the kids had someone watching out for the parents too. If they saw a parent headed in the direction of a couple who was slow dancing on a fast song, they promptly implemented the secret code

POW (Parent on the Way). Whoever saw a parent coming would scream: "POW!" and everyone at the party would join in and repeatedly shout "POW!" even louder, as if it was part of the song. That way, the guys knew to quickly pull away and pretend they were talking, not bumping and grinding. The parents probably knew what was going on, but they never caught anyone in the act, so the kids achieved their goal. The boys and girls continued with their sneaky kissing, bumping, and grinding until the party was over. *Now, those were the good old days when teenagers thought they knew more than their parents, not realizing that most parents had already been there and done that very thing that they thought was so exceptional.* Most teenagers think it is hilarious when parents say "been there, done that," to the point that they find no truth in the statement at all. As older folks used to say keep living and these things too shall come to pass. *Teenagers will be saying the same thing to their kids!*

Unfortunately, the phone episode didn't go as well. It wasn't easy convincing Shundra's mom to change the rules. Even though Marcus could talk to Shundra on the phone, the conversation was concise, *and everyone knows how time flies as you giggle and whisper sweet nothings in the ear of a teenager.* Fifteen minutes every day before 7:00 p.m., just wasn't enough time. And, her mom's friendly reminder didn't help the situation either.

Back in those days, there were no cell phones. The average household had Touch- Tone phones with a keypad to dial numbers and make phone calls. It was usually two of them: one for the living room or den area and one for the parents' room. It was the same phone line, so Shundra's mom could pick up the phone in her room while Shundra was talking on the phone in the living room or den and listen to her whole conversation if she desired.

Sometimes, she would pick up the other end of the phone and announce how much time Shundra had left to talk. It was embarrassing. Besides that, Shundra never knew what part of her conversation her mom heard, which was equally humiliating. But, she dared not say anything because she already knew what the response would be: "I pay the bills in this house! Everything here belongs to me! If you don't like my rules, LEAVE!"

It didn't seem fair because Marcus's parents' rules were different. He didn't have a time limit. He could talk on the phone for as long as he wanted until 9:30 p.m. Shundra was somewhat insecure because after speaking with Marcus for 15 minutes, he could be talking with some other girl for all she knew.

Shundra pleaded her argument, saying, "Mom, that's not enough time. We only had a few minutes to say hello and how are you doing, and that's all."

Her mom would respond, "You just used up five of those minutes arguing with me." And that's how it was: a dispute between opposing parties, needing to be resolved by a court. Mom was the judge, and Dad was the juror who agreed with everything her mom said. Before the ruling started, Shundra was already defeated. The judgment was, "Rules are rules," and there was no changing Mom's mind. So, Shundra used the last ten minutes whispering sweet nothings for the rest of the night and hoped the two of them made better use of their time the next day. Sarcastically, Shundra told Marcus to tell her everything he wanted to say at school or on the way home. He agreed, and they laughed about it together.

By the time Shundra reached the 10th grade, her mom officially allowed Marcus to come over from time to time. It was nice having him over watching TV, laughing and talking with the family. Girls braiding guys' hair was popular and part of the dating process during those days. Marcus had a good grade of hair, and Shundra didn't mind braiding it because it was an excuse for him to come over at least once a week.

Sometimes, more than braiding hair took place when no one was looking. Even with Mom's defense protocols like Marcus coming over only when she was home. Or, him being allowed only in the family room where family members regularly came in and out. And, Shundra's seven-year-old baby sister named Linda, invading their so-called privacy every time they would sit a little close together.

Linda would sneak around the corner, *probably instructed by Mom*, waiting to seize an opportunity to intrude, especially if the lights were off. She was annoying, but she wasn't always able to interrupt.

Marcus managed to slide his hand under Shundra's skirt and pleasantly indulge her with his fingers. Shundra had never experienced anything like that before. She didn't know what he was doing, but it felt good, and she liked the way her body reacted. *Boys! Why are they so mannish! How did he know to do such a thing; his curiosity or was he coached? And why did Shundra feel it was ok to let him? Of course, it was Marcus who said, "Nothing ever happened from two people holding hands." Really? You can't trust teenagers! This is the very reason some parents are strict with their children.*

Shundra had no problem walking home from school holding hands, going to the drive-in theatre, going to parties with Marcus, or letting him pleasantly indulge her with his fingers, but when it came to kissing, that was a whole different story.

When Marcus would try to kiss her, she would turn away. When he asked her to look at him, she couldn't find the courage to gaze her eyes into his. Finally, he asked her if she knew how to kiss, and she told him no. Of course, he smiled and said, "I will teach you." *Wow! She didn't mind Marcus's hands underneath her skirt, but she was afraid of her lips touching his. Seriously, what was she thinking?*

It so happened that on this day, while standing on the porch, Shundra agreed to experiment. And this time, she didn't have a problem gazing into Marcus's eyes. Her curiosity got the best of her, and she wanted to see Marcus's reactions as he talked her through the process of kissing.

Marcus told her as their lips get closer together, to open her mouth and put her tongue inside his mouth. She wanted to know what would happen next. He laughed and said, "You will see." Sharon, Shundra's sister who was a year younger, was standing behind the door listening to every word, so as Marcus slowly approached Shundra's lips, Sharon peeked from the side of the door and whispered, "Shundra, close your eyes." Since their mouths had just begun to touch, Shundra giggled and closed her eyes.

She felt a strange sensation, unexplained chills like goosebumps, and quickly pulled away. She didn't know if she liked it or not. She had a lot more saliva coming from her mouth than usual, and that was nasty to her. But at least now, she knew how to kiss and could decide whether or not she wanted to do it again later.

Like a typical teenage boy, Marcus did try to kiss her several times afterward, but he never forced or nagged her about it, and that made her feel special and even closer to him. Of course, he eventually got what he wanted, which was a sloppy, wet kiss, according to Shundra's description, but he was happy, and so was she!

After the first kiss, it was no secret that they were officially high school sweethearts, and everyone knew it. Shundra was now Marcus's girl, and he made sure he respected her as such. His buddies could not curse around her, and if they did, he would immediately put them in their place. He would say, "Don't you see my girl standing here?" Or, "Man, watch your mouth," and without hesitation, they'd begin to apologize and speak correctly. A few of the girls who hung out with his friends weren't so nice. They too had mouths like sailors, but that didn't matter to Marcus. If he felt they were out of line, he would tell his buddies, "Man, you better get your girl," and somehow they laughed it off without any confrontations or derogatory language after that.

Small things like Marcus standing up for her or speaking on her behalf made Shundra feel loved, protected, and unique. In return, she wanted him to feel her appreciation and the love that was emerging faster than her understanding. It was more than a teenage crush to Shundra. Even without sex, it was a sense of completeness that made her want to be a better soul mate to Marcus. Their relationship was like being in a sea of love, and it was the most beautiful and overwhelming feeling she had ever felt.

4

Trouble in Paradise

By the time she reached the 11th grade, the two of them had a strong bond they felt would last till the end of time. Little did they know, trouble was just around the corner for two teens that had just begun to experience life, love, and relationships! And so, the saga began.

Marcus was now a senior in high school with a 1965 Ford Mustang. The motor was so loud that Shundra could hear him coming two streets over before he actually made it to her house. It didn't matter if it was day or night because the sound of that motor was always the sunshine of her life. She enjoyed the heads-up that Marcus was close by, and she eagerly waited for him as she headed toward the front door, waiting to greet him. However, there was undoubtedly some truth in "all good things must come to an end." When you meet someone special, in the beginning, there are butterflies, then a week, a month, or even a year or two later, it just might all disappear, as it did in Marcus's and Shundra's case.

Soon she learned that Marcus had a crush on a girl who lived close by the grocery store where she worked part-time. That was the first encounter that Shundra had with Marcus seeing other girls. While she was working, she heard a loud vehicle that sounded much like Marcus's car. She thought he was coming to the store to visit her, but he never came inside. *Maybe that wasn't him*, she thought. But several days later, she heard the same sound again. *What were the odds of her suddenly hearing that same sound in the same week?*

Intuition led her to believe it was Marcus's car. But, she had to find out without a doubt before accusing him, so she did her own investigating. When she got off of work, she asked her ride home, to take her two streets down from the store. She said she wanted to pass down the road to see how close a coworker worked from the job. She was lying, of course, but her ride didn't know that.

Shundra had no idea where Marcus would be, but she knew she could hear his car two streets over before he got to her; so she took a chance and guessed what street he might be on. As they passed down the road, she saw Marcus's car and then she saw him!

He was standing on the front porch, face-to-face with this girl, with one arm pressed against the screen door, their bodies almost touching, and they were grinning from ear to ear like she and Marcus did whenever they were together. Her heart, covered in darkness, descended to a place where she thought it would never return. It felt like thorns pricking her heart's core existence that was about to explode. The pain was enormous, like nothing she had ever experienced before.

Because she wasn't driving, and since she had lied about why she wanted to come that way in the first place, she kept quiet. Silently, tears began to run down her cheeks. She turned her head and quickly wiped them away so her ride would not ask what was wrong.

There was no explanation Marcus could offer that would lift her heart beneath the surface. Still, when he called later that night, she confronted him, and of course, he denied it. But she knew what she had seen, and it shattered her heart into broken pieces. She envisioned rose petals falling one by one as she thought, *he loves me, he loves me not.*

It was getting close to Marcus's prom, an extraordinary day when she thought something expected and magical would happen. Now, she wasn't sure if he would ask her to go to his prom or not. It just didn't seem fair to her that after all of their years together, some other girl would be his date on his prom night.

She couldn't imagine why the sudden changes with Marcus were taking place, especially since she thought the two of them would someday be married. But the thought of marriage was now in despair and heading quickly to being impossible as Marcus continued enjoying his life with other girls.

Somehow, he managed to soothe her broken heart, and he did ask her to go to the prom. It turned out to be a very adorable night, as the two of them dressed elegantly in black and white, walking side by side, holding hands, and glowing in the spotlight. Like students do when thinking of who would most likely be their school's king and queen, Marcus and Shundra were among the adorable couples that year, and most likely to get married someday too! It was his prom and her night to shine. And for that moment, it was fabulous! It was like Shundra's dream had come true.

A few months after the prom, Shundra learned why the sudden change in Marcus. They had dated all through middle school and now in high school. They were high school sweethearts, and most of their friends thought they would be married. Marcus's brothers thought so too, but they advised him to date other girls before thinking of marriage. They said to him, "We know you love Shundra; you know you love Shundra, and you know Shundra is the girl you will marry. We want

24

you to experience life before settling down. Once you tie the knot, brother, that's it…your girl for life!"

Marcus evidently felt his brothers had a valid point and started dating other girls almost immediately. His weekend visits were fading away. Marcus's response to Shundra when she asked if he was coming over became a maybe, instead of a definite, "I will see you tonight." Their phone conversations were short and sweet instead of all night long of how much I enjoy being with you; how much I love you; and just wait until we get married.

Everything had suddenly changed right before Shundra's eyes, and she had no idea of how to get Marcus wrapped around her heart again. It was an unfamiliar game to her that people played all the time, and she did not like it at all.

It didn't help that Shundra's parents were still a little strict with her dating Marcus. On Saturday nights, visiting hours were over by 9:00 p.m., which gave Marcus a lot of freedom to come and go as he pleased after visiting Shundra. It wasn't long before another thorn began pricking at Shundra's heart.

Marcus met a cute girl who lived three streets over from where Shundra lived. Dolly was her name. She attended a different school than most kids in the neighborhood, and Shundra didn't know her very well. But, like always, the sound of Marcus's car gave his little secret away. One could hear the loud motor of his car whenever he was nearby, and some of Shundra's friends confirmed when they saw Marcus's car at Dolly's house.

The flame did not last very long with Dolly and Marcus. Besides, Marcus never admitted to ever having a relationship with her anyway. But, shortly after it supposedly ended, the word was out that Marcus was seeing a different girl across town. This girl lived in Stafford Westside; a neighborhood Shundra never dared to visit. The game Marcus was playing increased to a whole different level, and that was the start and the end of Marcus and Shundra's future relationship.

There were many rumors of fighting and killing happening in that neighborhood, and those who lived in the Rosie Dale subdivision, where Shundra lived, did not mix well. But, Shundra didn't care at the time; she wanted to see where Marcus was hanging out.

Shundra was fortunately acquainted with three brothers that looked like Mandingo men: big, tall, black, and muscular. They had muscles popping out from their eyebrows to their pinkie toe, like how Steve Harvey described all Mandingo men. The brothers fit the profile, which was exactly the image Shundra wanted them to portray. It just so happened that they owned the new franchise restaurant where Shundra was now working, and they treated her like their little sister. She convinced one of the brothers, named David, to take her into this neighborhood to find Marcus. Naturally, she didn't tell him everything. *Yeah, whenever Marcus was involved, not only did she play private investigator, but Shundra had become a natural-born liar too!*

David probably wouldn't have taken her had he known what she was planning. She only told him enough to get what she wanted because she knew he would protect her, if necessary. Shundra had driven down the girl's street a few times on her own before, hoping to catch Marcus in action. Fortunately for Marcus and Shundra, she never did. She didn't see Marcus's car, so she didn't know the exact house where the girl lived.

It didn't matter this particular day because Marcus's best friend, Jerome, mentioned the girl's name by mistake. Shundra intentionally said to him that she was going to Stafford Westside, and immediately he laughed and said, "You going to catch Marcus at Tamara's?"

26

Shundra's response was, "Oh, so that's the girl's name!

Jerome said, "Oh, shit!"

He'd just confirmed Shundra's suspicion that Marcus would be in the area. Even though Shundra didn't know the address and Jerome wasn't going to tell her now, she knew Marcus's car, and that was enough for her.

Shundra was hoping to catch Marcus in action because she didn't know when she would get another opportunity to have a bodyguard by her side. Lucky for her, as they were driving down Tamara's street, she saw Marcus's car parked at the fifth house on the left-hand side; and there he was, standing on the porch talking with her, just like the first time she saw him with another girl. And this time, she wasn't going for just passing by.

Shundra got out of the car and started walking towards Marcus. As soon as he recognized it was her, he came running, shouting, "Shundra, what are you doing here? Go home! These people don't play! You don't want to mess with them!"

He was right. She didn't want to mess with them. The problem wasn't them; it was him. So she got in his face and talked as much noise as she possibly could as Tamara stood there and watched. Marcus was fussing while forcing Shundra toward the car. He was looking over his shoulders like he knew something was about to happen to Shundra. And he didn't want that!

David, her Mandingo bodyguard, didn't say a word. He just stood there leaning against the car, watching every move Marcus made, anticipating what he would do if he or anyone tried to hurt Shundra. Finally, Marcus convinced Shundra to leave. Neither Marcus nor David said a word to one another. Shundra got in the car with David, and they left.

David wasn't pleased with Shundra's actions. He said it was a foolish thing to do; then he continued to explain the position she had put him and herself in. David scolded her like a father would do a ten-year-old child. And, he told her don't ever get him tangled up in a lover's quarrel again.

Needless to say, the ride home was not pleasant. Shundra couldn't say a word because she knew she was wrong. Later, she apologized and explained how her emotions simply exploded into action when she found out Marcus was cheating. She told David she wasn't trying to cause trouble for him, but she was afraid to go alone and reacted without thinking of what could or might happen.

David accepted her apology, but their relationship was never the same afterward, and that made her feel very uncomfortable around him. But, there was nothing she could do about it, except let time take its course.

5

The Nemesis That Would Not Quit

Despite all that happened, Tamara still became the thorn embellished in Shundra's side. She was the nemesis that would not quit. Her sneaky and charming personality mesmerized Marcus. Everyone believed she was a sweet little angel, while she deviously sabotaged everything belonging to Shundra. She was sneaky as a snake, striking from the shadows whenever she felt threatened. Then, she would sit back to see what would happen while pretending her disturbing ways were non-existence.

Shundra described Tamara as a sociopathic liar and a hypocrite. Like when she pretended to be Shundra and called her job saying she was sick and could not come to work. Now, imagine how surprised and perplexed Shundra's manager was when Shundra showed up ready and able to work. He had already arranged for someone else to work in her place. Shundra was a diligent worker, and she needed her money, but her manager had no other choice but to send her home. Because of Tamara's devious ways, Shundra had to make do with a small paycheck for the week. *Messing with someone's lively-hood is never a good thing!*

Tamara's compulsive lying appeared again when she told Shundra's friend LaToya that Shundra had been talking about her behind her back. Shundra was enraged. She and LaToya were close as two peas in a pod. They shared secrets, partied together, discussed relationship issues; and sometimes, they planned stake-outs to catch their cheating boyfriends in the act. There was no reason for Shundra to talk about LaToya to Tamara. Their friendship was solid as a rock as they faced many obstacles together, and most of them concerned their boyfriends.

LaToya's boyfriend was good-looking, and girls followed him around as if he was a sheep leading the herd to pasture. And, just like Marcus, when asked about his wrongdoings, he would lie and say, "It wasn't me. I didn't do it." So, LaToya's and Shundra's hands were full trying to figure out when, where, and who they would find with their cheating boyfriends. It wasn't enough that Tamara already had Marcus, she wanted Shundra's friends as well, or at least destroy the friendship Shundra had with them. Tamara had a very infamous personality!

Marcus made his decision, and there wasn't much Shundra could do about it, so she tried to move on with her life. But every which way she turned, Tamara was interfering, trying to claim Marcus as hers and lying to gain his trust. *Unfortunately for Shundra, she succeeded.*

Slowly, Shundra began to venture outside her comfort zone to meet other guys, but her heart still belonged to Marcus. She wanted nothing more than for Marcus to attend her prom as her boyfriend, her sweetheart, and hopefully, her future husband. But with Tamara in the picture, she wasn't sure that would ever happen since Marcus didn't seem to be interested in going with her. Marcus was once like a special red rose, representing an unchanging love that would never wither away. He meant everything to Shundra. *But, if she was ever a rose to him, it was evident that she had become a fungus; and the love, like the rose petals, were swiftly falling off.*

Shundra was maturing and learning that love had many splendors, but often they come and go. She needed to focus on finding someone else to escort her to her prom since Marcus may not be the one.

And undeniably, just like a typical male would do, Marcus was still testing the waters with Shundra. He was trying to eat his cake and have it too. For a long time after Tamara won Marcus's heart, he was still calling and visiting Shundra from time to time, and that made it harder for her to let go of him entirely.

6

Losing Her Virginity

Forest Lake was the most popular park and recreation for family reunions, picnics, and swimming. Often, teenagers gathered there to make out and have some fun of their own. And, it was there, where Shundra almost lost her virginity.

In the midst of trying to win Marcus's love, *because she couldn't leave him alone*, Shundra agreed to go riding with him. He wanted to talk and explain where they were in their relationship. Shundra knew this would probably be an emotional time for her, but she had no idea it would be sensitive for Marcus as well.

He drove to Forest Lake and parked in a secluded area. Suddenly, as they were talking, the mood changed and tears ran down both their faces. Marcus reached over to wipe the tears from Shundra' chin, then he planted tiny kisses on her face for each tear he wiped away. With each kiss, he repeated, "I'm sorry, baby. I didn't mean to hurt you." It sounded so genuine that Shundra thought to herself, *how will I ever get over him?* Again, he kissed her lips, and she reciprocated. The heartfelt gesture was so real that Shundra forgot about all the thorns Marcus caused that were still piercing her heart.

Slowly, he put his hand under her blouse and began to move it over her head gently. She did not resist. It felt scorching in the car as the windows started to fog. It was so romantic, and at that moment, Shundra felt like Marcus belonged to her and only her. Although it seemed like a lifetime ago, it was the moment Shundra was waiting on.

Marcus reached behind Shundra's back to unsnap her bra when someone knocked on the window. It was a policeman! Shundra grabbed her blouse and put it on as fast as she could. The policeman tapped on the glass, and Marcus rolled down the window. "What are you kids doing here? the policeman asked.

"Just talking, Marcus said.

"Well, talk somewhere else, the policeman replied. It's against the law to sit in the park with your clothes off.

"Yes, sir, Officer! We are leaving right now!" said Marcus.

Because of the speed limit, Marcus drove slowly through the park. He did not want the policeman to revisit him for speeding. During the ride, Marcus and Shundra did not say a word to one another. When Marcus reached the main road, he quickly drove Shundra home.

Some time afterward, Marcus and Shundra were able to laugh over their experience. It was a pretty funny ordeal, but unfortunately, the episode did not change their situation. Marcus was still with Tamara, and Shundra realized that no matter what, their life together would never be the same. *Shundra drew to Marcus like a drug addict.* There was no way she could stop herself cold turkey. She decided to talk with him whenever she could, but leave the door of her heart open for other possibilities. *That was a smart decision!*

Still, Shundra was vulnerable and hopeful that they would get back together. So, when Marcus came over and spent most of the day with her, she was delighted. Then, Marcus decided they would stop by his brother's apartment. It wasn't by coincidence; he knew they would be there alone. Self-consciously, Shundra told herself, *"Oh, no! Sex, don't do it!"* But she ignored the warning and willingly laid across the bed. *Again, Marcus comes to her; and without hesitation, she walks right into his arms.* It was months later, but this time, she did lose her virginity. *She probably thought she would win back his heart with sexual intimacy since it was one thing they had never done.*

Marcus laid beside her and gazed at her beauty, and for the moment, they did nothing but look at one another. Then, he kissed her forehead, and Shundra smiled. Without a word, Marcus slowly undressed her. As his hands gently touched her breast, he told her it was his first time too; but she didn't believe him. *Something was keeping him from totally committing.* Marcus fondled between her legs and told her he felt like she was ready. Shundra wondered why he made such a statement. She was ready the minute she decided to let him proceed. But, she smiled and said, "Ok."

Marcus was very gentle, but it still hurt as he inserted himself inside her. She wiggled her way across the other side of the bed. "Where are you going?" he asked.

All she would say was, "It hurts."

His response was, "I'm sorry, baby, it's very tight." *Sex, an overrated act in Shundra's mind!* Nothing about it was as impressive as she thought it would be. It wasn't magical, and it didn't feel like they were bonding at all, especially when she saw blood on the sheets.

Shundra was not expecting blood, so she wondered what Marcus did to her. She told him something was seriously wrong. But, Marcus said no, it wasn't. He said that his older brother told him girls always bleed the first time. Marcus promised Shundra that it wouldn't be so bad the next time. *As if there was going to be "the next time,"* she

34

thought.

Inside the walls of her vagina seemed so irritated that she could hardly walk. All she wanted to do was sit in a warm tub of water and hope it was soothing.

Marcus ran the bath water. As they bathed together, he kissed the back of her neck and held her very close. Then, he dried her off, helped her get dressed, and they left the apartment. Weeks passed before Shundra spoke to Marcus again.

The intimacy they shared did seem to bring them a little closer. But, Tamara knew how to compete and she was very good at it. *She was probably no virgin and knew how to excite Marcus, which was something Shundra knew nothing about.*

Whatever she was doing, it had Marcus's nose wide open. Not only was he curious and eager for more of Tamara, but his heart seemed attached to her as well. Shundra felt disconnected to Marcus more and more every day.

7

A Date She Will Never Forget

Tick tock, tick tock, tick tock, the sound of the clock interrupted Shundra's bittersweet memories. Shortly afterward, the alarm went off, and she stretched her arms out as far as she could across the bed, trying to reach the button to shut it off.

She looked at the clock and thought to herself, *Hum, a few extra minutes to lie there.* But reality quickly sets in, and she remembered that she was driving Deanna and herself to work. They work for J. Harrison and Associates, a recruiting firm founded in 2005 that built their success on the ability to place candidates with employers of like minds permanently.

Since the gas prices were skyrocketing, and the two of them didn't live far from one another, they decided to carpool and save a few bucks. Their hours were flexible, so time wasn't crucial, but Deanna didn't like reporting to work later than 8:30 a.m. Therefore, Shundra had to hustle to get dressed and over to Deanna's by 7:45 a.m. When she arrived, Deanna was standing by the door, smiling and waiting as usual. "Right on time," she said sarcastically.

Shundra smiled back with her usual response, "Like always."

For the first time, while on their way to work, small talk revealed how much sadness the two of them had in common. "My life was like thorns and roses: love and loss, heartaches and pain," said Shundra. *Of course, Shundra is referring to Marcus and Tamara.* She labeled Marcus as the guy she loved and lost; and Tamara as the girl who caused her the most heartaches and pain.

Then, suddenly, Shundra's facial expression changed from a confident and secure look to loss and contempt. *She was about to share another thorn in her life. And this one, she had not talked about since the incident happened.* "I remembered feeling empty and determined to get over Marcus," she said. "I agreed to go out with my friend Belinda and her boyfriend, Brandon, and a friend of his whom I did not know. Belinda was fascinated with Brandon's age, and she was crazy in love with him." *Like Shundra is with Marcus.*

Brandon had not seen John for many years. He was excited to run across an old friend. He wanted John to meet Belinda, and to catch up on how things were with him and his family. So, he invited John to join him and Belinda later on that evening. Brandon thought it would be a great ideal if Belinda had a friend to go along and make it a double date. He told John he would ask Belinda if one of her friends wanted to join them and let him know later.

"When Belinda approached me, she presented the idea as meeting someone new to help me get my mind off Marcus. My first thought was *sure, why not? After all, that was the idea. I did want to meet other guys to get over Marcus so that I could move on with my life.*

She told me it was her first time meeting Brandon's friend too, but she trusted Brandon's judgment of character and said she thought he would be ok to meet. She told me we were going to the family's clubhouse for teens to listen to music and have a few drinks. The club

37

was closed for the weekend while Brandon's parents were away on vacation.

"That evening, I rode with Brandon and Belinda to the clubhouse, and John met us there later. When I first saw him, I knew he was much older than I initially thought he would be; but good-looking, and he seemed to be nice too. Brandon introduced him first to Belinda and then to me. We all laughed and talked for a few minutes before Brandon turned on the music and brought in the drinks. Everything was going well until Brandon and Belinda decided to disappear somewhere on the premises for privacy.

"I wondered why Belinda would leave me alone with a total stranger. Trying not to be too cynical, I rekindled my feelings in hopes of having a great evening without thinking of Marcus.

"I could hear Belinda and Brandon laughing, playing, and having a good time as I sat quietly with nothing to say to John. His conversation was boring, and worst of all, he was beginning to ignore my boundaries. And that made me feel very uncomfortable.

"It started with him putting his arm around my shoulder, and then he aggressively tried to kiss me. 'No, I'm not kissing you!' I said as I abruptly pushed him away. He didn't ask why not, nor did he back away.

"Nobody turns me down, he said. 'You don't know what you are missing. Girls think I am a great kisser.'

"I was disgusted with his behavior! I frowned, and said, 'That may be true, but I don't kiss guys on the first day I meet them.' Still, he wouldn't stop. He tried to force me into doing something I did not want to do.

"Suddenly, I felt his hands on my boobs, as if he was trying to squeeze them. I screamed very loud, trying to get Belinda's and

Brandon's attention.

"He was much stronger than I realized. I couldn't get away from him. He put his hand over my mouth and pushed me against the table, and started rubbing on my jeans as if he was trying to find the zipper. I felt defenseless.

"My legs and feet were the only things I could use to fight back as I tried to getaway. My upper body was pinned tightly against the table, so I kicked as hard as I could.

"The kicking knocked over a chair, and suddenly Brandon and Belinda came running into the room. Brandon pulled John off me and said, 'Man! What the hell are you doing?'

"John shouted, "Man, I'm sorry! I'm sorry!"

"Belinda grabbed me and put her arms around me. "Are you all right?' she asked. I was crying so hard that I could not answer with words, so I nodded to let her know I was ok. Brandon made John leave the clubhouse.

"Then, Brandon apologized to me for his friend's behavior. Brandon made sure I was all right before he took me home. He didn't understand what was going on with John.

"Brandon continued to apologize, saying he would never have asked John to come had he known he would try and do anything against my will. I could see how disturbing this was for Brandon and that he was trying to get to the root of things.

"Brandon wanted to know if I had led John on in any way. I told him, "No, he acted like a madman who felt he could take what he wanted, even though I told him no many times.'

"Later, Brandon learned why he had not seen John in such a long time. As it turned out, John was in prison for eight years for armed robbery and released three days before Brandon saw him. No one mentioned to Brandon John's conviction or the time he received for his crime. Brandon thought John moved from the neighborhood like everyone else and was visiting when they saw one another. He felt it was coincidental that their path crossed, and he was glad to see his old friend.

"Maybe, their conversation would have been a lot different had he known," said Shundra. Deanna was astonished. She was listening to Shundra's story, visualizing the scene, and relating to her very own personal experience. Shundra's story brought out a different set of emotions for Deanna than it did when she's watching this type of stuff on TV.

Shundra turned into the parking garage and parked the car. As they were gathering their belongings, Deanna said, "That was an awful thing to have happened to you. Did something recently occur to make you think about this? she asked.

"No. I was reminiscing about my past, and while chronologically recalling the experiences I had, that one suddenly invaded my mind, Shundra said. It wasn't something I was proud of, but I recognized it as reality. Then, she smiled, and said, I'm not sure why I shared it with you, but hopefully you will keep this information between you and me.

"Of course, I will, said Deanna.

Deanna had a similar story to share, so she was glad Shundra trusted her with hers. "Let's go to Brown's BBQ today for lunch, Deanna suggested. "It's a great spot to enjoy good food and have a little privacy too.

"Okay. Let me check my schedule, and I will let you know for sure if I am available. I will call you 30 minutes ahead of time to confirm, said Shundra.

"Okay, said Deanna. Let's try for 1:00 p.m. after the lunch crowd has come and gone."

The timing was perfect because Shundra managed to get all her calls in before lunch, so they went to Brown's BBQ.

After placing their orders, Deanna told Shundra that she had a similar story from the past that she wanted to share. "Believe it or not, I am a victim of incest," she said. Shundra tried hard not to show any facial expressions so Deanna wouldn't know what she was thinking, *John, someone I didn't know, and who almost raped me was bad enough, but a relative is more devastating than I can imagine.*

"It happened a long time ago too, back when families said, "what happened in the household, stayed in the household," said Deanna. 'I wanted to talk with someone open-minded about the situation, someone who wasn't judgmental. You are the first person that I've told. After hearing your story, I felt I could share it with you."

Shundra nodded her head as if to say, *"Ok, I understand."* Because of her experience, she knew how hard it was to open up and talk about such an ordeal.

"I was 12 years old when my father approached me and said he wanted to teach me about boys. He didn't go into many details. We were very close, and I had no reason to distrust him. He said he would come and get me when he was ready. Weeks went by before he approached me again. This time, it was in the middle of the night when everyone was asleep. All, he said was, 'Come with me.' And I did. He took me to the garage, and we got inside the back seat of the car. I was wearing a short nightgown, which made it easy for him to start touching me inappropriately because the gown fit loosely and covered nothing for protection. I don't remember why I didn't know it was wrong. Nor do I remember if I fully understood that private parts of my body were

41

off-limits. Besides, he was my father who loved me and would never do anything wrong to hurt me, so I thought.

"It felt strange, but it was something new to me, so I thought it was supposed to feel the way that it did. I don't recall being in any pain, just uncomfortable. When it was over, I went back to bed. About a month later, in broad daylight when I was home alone, it happened again. This time, he took me to my parents' bedroom, undressed me, and inserted himself inside of me as far as it would go without force.

I recalled another time when everyone but my mom was home that he quietly closed the bedroom door, locked it, and proceeded the same as before: inserting himself inside me without force. It was happening so often that I didn't want to learn anything else about boys! I began to withdraw from his presence. I would go in a different direction when I thought he was looking my way. Or, I would make sure I was with my siblings whenever he was around. Still, he found a way to continue doing what he was doing.

Finally, I decided to tell my mom, who didn't believe me initially. Months passed, and I still had to endure this unspeakable act, and I was sick of it.

My teacher noticed that my focus was elsewhere during class, which was unusual because I was a scholar in math. I loved to participate and compete with my classmates; but for some reason, I wasn't doing either. One day as I was leaving class, my math teacher stopped me. She asked if something was bothering me. She said she was available to talk if I needed her.

I was surprised that she noticed my despair; and at the same time, I remembered the household rule: What happens in the household, stays in the house. So, I told my teacher 'no, nothing was going on with me.' Maybe it was the way I answered, or perhaps it

42

was the look on my face when I answered; either way, my teacher did not accept my response. Instead, she insisted that I tell her what was going on. I told her that I couldn't say because I would get in trouble if I did. Naturally, to win my trust, she said she wouldn't tell anyone unless I wanted her too." *Deanna's teacher was in for a surprise, but she liked Deanna and was willing to do almost anything to help her.*

I felt I could trust my teacher, so I informed her of everything, including how often it was happening. She was outraged. She said, 'Deanna, I know I said that I would not tell anyone; but what your father is doing is wrong, and it has to stop! I'm afraid the only way to get him to stop is to report him.' I was hysterical. I cried and pleaded for my teacher to leave it alone, to keep it to herself as she promised. I said, 'No, please don't report him. I don't want him to get in trouble, and I don't want to get in trouble either.' She tried to calm me down, but I told her I was lying. 'I promise you; I am lying!' I said. Then, I screamed, 'You are lying too, and that's what I will tell anyone if anyone asks me!'

My teacher saw how upset I was becoming, so she decided to offer me some comforting words instead. That way, she had time to figure out how to handle the situation. She asked me if I had read the Serenity Prayer. The calmness of her voice was beginning to calm me down. I wiped my face and said no. She told me whenever there was a problem that she could not immediately resolve, she would read this prayer to help her make it through the day. She had read it so much that she had it memorized. So, she got a pen and some paper, and she wrote:

The Serenity Prayer

God grant me the serenity
to accept the things I cannot change;

Courage to change the things I can;
And, wisdom to know the difference.
Living one day at a time;
Enjoying one moment at a time;
Accepting hardships as the pathway to peace;
Taking, as He did, this sinful world
As it is, not as I would have it;
Trusting that He will make all things right
If I surrender to His Will;
So that I may be reasonably happy in this life
And supremely happy with Him
Forever and ever in the next.

Amen.

She gave the prayer to me and told me, 'When you feel discouraged or defeated; I want you to read this!' I told her that I would, and then, I thanked her for not saying anything to anyone. My teacher smiled playfully, knowing her being quiet was not the right thing to do; but, she needed to buy some time to figure out a way to help without me feeling betrayed.

As time passed, I began to act like myself once again. It was like the weight of carrying a secret for such a long time lifted from my broken spirit. And things at home did get better. I don't know whether my mom questioned my dad or not, but he decided to back off. And, I was happy to get rid of the guilt of trusting him and thinking there was nothing wrong with what he was doing. Finally, I could live as normal girls should. But, things were never the same for my dad or me again. We still had somewhat of a relationship, but nothing like it was before when I considered us as close."

Shundra listened to Deanna's story without interruption. She could feel the agony that she was still struggling with, even though it happened a very long time ago. She was hoping since Deanna was able to release it, she could move forward without the sorrow. *Sometimes by sharing one's own experience, good or bad, it helps others understand they are not alone; some have experienced the same thing or worse and have successfully made it through some of life's hardest struggles.*

Shundra gave Deanna a gentle and long hug, and the two of them sat there quietly for a moment or two. They spent an hour and a half talking, and now they had to rush back to work.

Shundra told Deanna, "If you ever need to talk, please know that I am always here for you, ok?"

Deanna was thankful that Shundra could relate to the situation.

"You are a blessing, she said. 'Thank you so much for listening and understanding.' Then, they hugged once again and parted in different directions heading to their cars.

8

The Two Admirers

After work, Shundra took Deanna home, and then she met Gayle at DEC for class. For once, Shundra was on time, and Gayle couldn't believe it. Gayle was now with the advanced level and on a different dance floor. Shundra was still with the intermediate group, so in passing, she smiled at Gayle as she walked to the back corner of the dance floor. It was her favorite spot because she thought her shy personality would go unnoticed in the corner where no one was watching. But, her two admirers knew just where to find her, every time.

Jordon was a stylish bald man with a beautiful silver beard and mustache. The smell of his cologne was so alluring that she wanted to lay her head on his chest and dance the night away. The shade of his skin was like light chocolate and butter pecan, which sparked her appetite. His eyes glittered with charm as he gazed into hers while they twisted and turned into the dance moves called out by the instructor, "Side basic, she turns, he turns, alternative walk, and sway."

"Shundra, you are good at this, Jordon said.

Shundra begins to blush. She looked downward and replied,

"Really? I feel like I have two left feet.

"Keep coming, and soon you will be doing the steps without thinking about it, just naturally following the rhythm, said Jordon, to which Shundra replied, 'I certainly hope so.'

Jordon continued with the compliments, especially when she completed a step correctly. He encouraged her to practice consistently.

Shundra wasn't sure if Jordon was interested in her or not, but she enjoyed dancing with him. It made her feel like a pro, and it put her shy personality at ease. Besides, the man was sophisticated, mysterious, and appeared to be very discreet — all three qualities in a man that Shundra loved.

Shundra was a classy woman who wanted a sophisticated man and was optimistic about Jordon's feelings. He appeared to have an adventurous personality, and Shundra liked trying different things. But most important, of the three qualities, was discreetness: whatever happened behind closed doors would remain behind those doors amongst her and her lover, especially if it was anyone from DEC.

However, Jordan proved he was not the man for her. Every week, when it was time for the open floor, which started at 9:00 p.m., Jordon disappeared from dancing altogether. His charisma didn't go unnoticed; other ladies were looking for him as well. Many were asking if anyone had seen Jordon. The response from most was no. But on one of those occasions, a lady said to us, "Jordon is married, with a family living in Atlanta. He was planning to move them here soon, so maybe he's not attending class anymore." Shundra was in shock because she didn't notice a ring on his finger. All fantasies and hopes of the two of them ever getting together quickly vanished.

So, next on Shundra's list of possibilities was Justin, who was also bald, around 5 feet, 6 inches tall, with dark skin. His smile was

47

gorgeous, and his teeth were a pearly white, which seemed to shine with delight whenever he approached her. He was always dressed to impress and was pleasing to the eyes, but Shundra wasn't sure what he was all about.

Justin knew the women at DEC were checking him out. He had this air that made one think he was probably saying to himself, "Damn, I look good." After all, this was a social setting for the grown and sexy. Ladies weren't afraid to make the first move, and Justin welcomed the invitations.

However, no matter what was happening with the other ladies, Justin always found his way to Shundra. He danced once or two with her before she was tired and ready to quit. Often, he gave her a break while he danced with the other ladies, but Justin always returned to Shundra when he felt she was ready to start again. Like Jordon, Justin was easy to dance with, and Shundra enjoyed dancing with him too.

Justin appeared to be in a great conversation with the guys, but his eyes were continually facing in Shundra's direction. If she happened to look his way, that gorgeous smile of his appeared instantly. That's all Justin needed: a glimpse from her that confirmed she was interested in him too!

Shundra could tell when Justin was talking about her because all the guys were looking at her too. She wondered what he was saying to them. *He's probably saying, "Man, look at her!"* Suddenly, her shy personality surfaced, and Shundra turned and looked in the opposite direction because she didn't like the stares.

But, that didn't stop Justin. On several occasions, he grabbed her by the arm and took her where the guys were standing and said, "Look at this pretty lady." Then, he had the nerve to ask, 'isn't she pretty, y'all?' Shundra wasn't happy with his behavior because it put her in the spotlight, and she couldn't find her way out. It was flattering, but also embarrassing.

9

The Idea of Thorns and Roses

Eleven o'clock always came too fast, and Gayle and Shundra had to leave to prepare for work the next day. After a long day of working and dancing during the weeknights, Gayle and Shundra were exhausted every time. They were satisfied and stress-free but tired. Shundra had no trouble falling asleep when she made it home, and she slept like a baby.

The next day, at work, her mind wandered back to her relationships in the good old days of flirting and hating as a young girl, and now, as an adult. As she recalled, each of her relationships commenced as roses, but most of them turned into a rose-thorn. Little did she know, punctured rose-thorns could cause Ulcers. It was like someone with a broken heart caused by cheating, no commitment, incompatible, incomprehensive communication, and low or no libido. And most of all, the absence of knowing and understanding love languages (gifts, words of affirmation, quality of time, acts of service, or physical touch as written and explained by Gary Chapman. Each of these instances played an enormous part in ingraining thorns throughout Shundra's life.

Suddenly, she thought! *Maybe I should start a journal of all the personalities and experiences I had with guys: the good, the bad, and the ugly. Who knows, it can turn out to be a good book or movie someday! After all, my recollection as a young girl so far includes Bobby, who was amusing; Roderick, who was absurd; Marcus, who was inconsiderate; Kevin, who was scandalous; John, who was criminal; Jordan, who was intriguing; and Justin, who was shameless. The book will feature the idea that "trouble don't last always" because the future has a way of overcoming the past. Or, for those who don't believe in overcoming the past, the book will be very amusing!*

She phoned Gayle to share her idea. Gayle was happy; however, since Shundra knew all about her and her secrets, she had one stipulation. "None of my intimacies, no matter what or how freaky goes in that book! she said.

"Even if I use an alias? Shundra asked.

"What part of 'no matter what' don't you understand? Gayle replied.

"But, your experiences will inspire others, especially women like me, that haven't found that guy who acts out fantasies and welcomes the enthusiasm when I tell him what makes my body react. These days, guys are so insecure, she said. They don't understand that sometimes, women want to explore the possibilities. They feel like we are criticizing their act of passion when they are told, touch me here or there, or do this or that. Your experiences give others hope and help us realize that we are not alone in wanting more from a man. What's wrong with that? Shundra asked.

"Shundra, I will sue the hell out of you! I'm not playing. Nothing I told you goes in that book, said Gayle.

Gayle wasn't falling for any of that "for a good cause" excuse Shundra was giving her. So, Shundra laughed and said, "Bye, girl!"

10

The Journaling Begins

Shundra took her laptop to her car and began to type everything she previously thought of, about Bobby, Roderick, Marcus, Kevin, John, Jordon, and Justin. Now, she had everything up to date and saved on her computer. Because of her workload and her dance classes, the best time to start writing for the book was during her lunch break. She couldn't wait to get started. She began typing precisely after the ordeal with John.

Monday - Lunch at 2:00 p.m.

The rape ordeal, coupled with the reality of losing Marcus, demoralized her, she typed. How could she get over Marcus by dating other guys if she was now afraid something like this could happen again? She wondered had she misled John in any way. If so, it wasn't intentional, and she didn't recall giving any mixed signals.

She intended to get away from her usual routine so she could meet someone other than Marcus. Double dating seemed like a good idea. *So, why not? Admittedly, there's no harm in that!* she thought. Her mind was cloudy and filled with confusion. Still, she needed to move on with her life, and she wondered who the next significant person in her life would be.

Several months later, the mystery unfolded along the trails of Forest Lake. She and her neighborhood friend, Deloris, were slowly walking the trails when they saw two guys jogging and quickly approaching them. On the left side was a dark, tall, slender, and bowlegged guy who was facing Deloris. The guy on the right side was not as tall. He was light-skinned, more of a medium height, and a little stout. He was facing Shundra. Without Deloris knowing why, before the guys were close enough to stop, Shundra switched sides. *This girl is on a mission. Meeting someone other than Marcus to occupy her time and to secure a date for her prom is her top priority.*

The slender, dark-skinned guy was pleasing to Shundra's eyes. The guys appeared to be on a mission as well. *Or maybe they are players and have come out to catch too, like Deloris and Shundra. Who knows?* They stopped and introduced themselves. "Hello, pretty lady."

"My name is Kenneth," said the one on the left who was now facing Shundra, since she switched sides. Shundra's eyes followed his eyes. He was checking her out from head to toe. By the time his eyes made it back to hers, his lips had formed the cutest grin that seemed to say, *"I like."* Shundra grinned back as if to say, *"I like too."* The other guy, on the right, followed Kenneth's lead and said to Deloris, "Hi, I'm Jason."

Shundra was too busy grinning at Kenneth to notice if Jason's smile was as mesmerizing as Kenneth's. Besides, Kenneth was the more talkative one, and Shundra was paying attention to his every word.

53

"What school do you all attend? asked Kenneth. He thought for a moment, then quickly said, 'Wait a minute, first, how old are you, pretty ladies?' Before either of them could answer, he asked several other questions, 'Are you all in high school? And what side of town do you all live?'

Deloris was quick to respond. She wasn't giving out all that information to strangers.

"The Northside, and what about you guys? she said.

Kenneth grinned, "We are from the Northside too. We graduated last year from Lakewood High.

Shundra grinned back. She was intrigued to know that they were out of high school and that they live on the same side of town. *She is a hot mama in the making! What does she know about older guys? Did she not learn anything from John, the jailbird, soon to be the sex offender?*

Jason said, "Well, ladies, we aren't going to detain you all any longer. We need to finish our run."

Kenneth agreed and offered to give Shundra his phone number, and she accepted. Jason gave Deloris his number as well. Slowly, they started to jog away; and while building up their momentum, Kenneth shouted, "Don't lose our numbers!"

Shundra shouted back, "We won't!

It was days later when Shundra called Kenneth. His voice was so masculine and sexy that it made her quiver. *His voice isn't all of that! Shundra is inexperienced, and Kenneth is far too advanced for her.*

Shundra could tell Kenneth was a sweet-talker because he said things she had not heard other guys say. *Silly girl! She doesn't know what she is getting involved in.* And, she liked what she was hearing because it felt better than sitting at home, crying over Marcus and

54

wondering if he was with Tamara.

Shundra turns 18 years old in three weeks, and she still needed a date for the prom. She wasn't going to find time to date if she didn't get out of Marcus's zone and the pity party she continued to indulge herself. So, for the moment, Kenneth's friendship was working fine, sweet-talking and all.

11

Plans for the Party

Shundra's parents agreed to have a backyard barbeque in celebration of her 18th birthday. Shundra was eager to invite Kenneth, especially since she wasn't sure if Marcus would come. Even if Marcus didn't come to the party, they shared the same friends, and Shundra knew

he would find out who was there. Childish as it may seem, Shundra wanted Marcus to realize he wasn't the only one seeing someone else. She wanted him to know the feeling of jealousy, the way she felt after learning of Tamara. *Here again, Shundra involves others in Marcus's and her disloyalties. When will she ever learn?*

Deloris invited Jason to come to the party as well. After several conversations over the phone, she had become quite fond of him.

Twenty-five of Shundra's classmates received invitations in the mail, and for the friends that lived on her street, she invited them personally. The total number of guests was 40, not including relatives.

The party was for Shundra's 18th birthday, but her mom decided it would be a party and a mini family reunion. The menu would be pork ribs, German sausages, chicken, and grilled pork chops with baked beans, potato salad, rolls, coleslaw, soda, and sweet tea. And, of course, the adult chaperons would have beer and liquor. The birthday cake was the only dessert on the menu.

Music, chairs, card tables, dominoes tables, and lights were set up in the backyard. The dance floor was the patio. The guests entered the party through the back gate only. That way, Shundra's mom and relatives would know who's coming in and out. NO ONE COULD GO INSIDE THE HOUSE WITHOUT PERMISSION! And, that was to use the restroom only, according to Shundra's mom.

12

Sweet Revenge

Three weeks later, the party started at 8:00 p.m. Four hours was on the invitations, so the curfew for the night was midnight. Marcus showed up around 11:00 p.m. *He probably couldn't get away from controlling Tamara.* But, it was perfect timing because Marcus saw Kenneth and Shundra in the same position as Shundra saw him and the other girl. They were face-to-face, with one arm pressing against the house, bodies almost touching and grinning from ear to ear. *Sweet revenge!*

He was standing across the street, talking with a friend and staring at Shundra, who went the extra mile to seem satisfied and happy. Shundra looked his way and smiled. He didn't crack a smile or say a word. He didn't look pleased with what he saw, so Marcus left as if he couldn't stand to see another guy with his girl.

Not a good look or a good feeling for a player! For the first time, Marcus showed remorse. He looked hurt like a jealous ex-boyfriend, and he played his role well. It was a small victory for Shundra as she celebrated her birthday, feeling positive that Marcus now understood the hurt she felt.

Two weeks later, Kenneth was visiting Shundra when she thought she heard Marcus's car. She peeked out the living room window but didn't see anything unusual. Shundra was sure she heard Marcus's car, so she peeked out the window ten minutes later and thought she saw him lurking around Kenneth's car.

She didn't see Marcus's car, but at a glance, she saw someone with a big afro in a white shirt. Although she didn't get a good look, she convinced herself that it was Marcus. *Who else would it be?* she thought. She didn't want Kenneth or Marcus fighting, so she didn't say anything. *No doubt, she's probably trying to protect Marcus. After all, he still has her heart.*

Shundra had no idea of the damage Marcus had done to Kenneth's car. When Kenneth was ready to leave, Shundra walked him outside. He noticed, almost immediately, that the two tires on the right-hand side of his car were flat. He stormed to the other side of the vehicle and found that those two tires were flat as well. In shock, he said, "What the hell happened to my car?"

Instantly, the uncertainty that Shundra felt about Marcus vanished. And now, she's too afraid to say what she saw. If Marcus was so over her, and so in love with Tamara, why would he do such a thing? she thought to herself.

Kenneth was furious. "When I find the MF"—trying to be respectful in front of Shundra—"who did this, I got something for his ass!" he said. Shundra continued to apologize, and Kenneth didn't understand why she was doing it.

"I am so sorry, and I feel horrible that this happened at my house," Shundra said.

"Shundra, don't worry about it. I am not upset with you," said Kenneth.

He walked around the car again, shaking his head, then he called a tow truck. Shundra could see the fire burning in his eyes. Her imagination was running wild with thoughts of what Kenneth would have done had he seen Marcus anywhere near his car.

But, at this point, Shundra's heart was with Kenneth. She wanted revenge against Marcus, but she didn't know Marcus would retaliate in such a horrible way.

The next day, Kenneth told Shundra that he purchased four new tires because the National Tire Company could not patch any of them. He said it cost him $800. *Now, that's what Marcus called sweet revenge! How dare him?* Shundra thought.

Shundra called Marcus to let him know that she saw him and that she knew what he did. He denied it, of course! And, said he was not lurking around her house. "I was with Tamara, and I can prove it." *Of course, he can; both Marcus and Tamara are liars!*

Shundra could hear the smirk in Marcus's voice, enjoying every bit of the disappointment he felt from her. She was intensely annoyed, as Kenneth continued to talk about the incident for days.

What a predicament, Shundra thought to herself. *I love Marcus with every drop of blood flowing through my veins; but what Marcus did was ruthless, especially since I am no longer his concern.* Shundra couldn't shake the feeling. Marcus's eyes and heart were on Tamara. *Why wasn't that enough? Why did he feel the need to sabotage Kenneth's car?* Such an act confused Shundra even more, and she wasn't sure if Marcus still loved her or not.

Marcus felt he had gotten away with it, apparently because a month later Kenneth's car was once again in Shundra's driveway, tires flat. He did show a little decency this time; he only cut one tire, and thankfully, Kenneth didn't have to replace it. *Really? Decency is to*

60

move on with his life, and leave Shundra and Kenneth alone! That's the respect Shundra was trying to show him and Tamara. Even with a broken heart, she loved Marcus enough to walk away so he could be happy. *Seriously, who is Shundra trying to fool? She could care less about Tamara. Marcus left her with no other choice but to walk away.* Still, she thought, Marcus couldn't eat his cake and have it too. She wondered why he couldn't see that.

Again, Kenneth was furious and ready to work off his frustration on that scum: the person who kept putting his tires flat. He wondered, *what was this person trying to accomplish?* "Do you have a secret admirer who doesn't want me around you? Or better yet, do you have an ex-boyfriend who wants you back?" Kenneth asked.

Shundra laughed and said, "No, not that I know of. You are the only person occupying my time these days. Maybe, it's one of my sisters' friends. I will ask if any of them are having problems with their boyfriends. It's possible that whoever is doing this, thinks your car is one of my sisters' friends. Who knows?" *Stop! Please stop lying for Marcus! He deserves a good ASS-whipping! Then, maybe he will leave that dude's car alone!*

Kenneth was feeling the need to set a trap for this scum. Or, maybe stop visiting Shundra. The uncertainties cross Shundra's mind as well. *Should I tell Kenneth it's Marcus? Or should I break things off with Kenneth? If Marcus promises to commit to me, breaking things off with Kenneth isn't a problem,* she thought. "This is so confusing to me," she whispers to herself.

Then, she remembered, *I still need a prom date. There is no way I'm giving up my date without a definite and meaningful response from Marcus.*

Kenneth decided to stay in the picture for a while. "You are worth the fight, baby. I'm not giving you up that easy," Kenneth said.

Shundra smiled with enthusiasm, thinking this man knows what to say to a girl! *He is probably pretending to stay in the picture, so he can catch the low-down dirty scum in the act. That way, he can give him that ASS-whipping he so deserves. Way to go, Kenneth!*

13

Dangerously Trying to Win Him Back

Marcus was in the neighborhood from time to time visiting his friend Byron who lived across the street from Shundra. Shundra had an opportunity to dress to impress Marcus for a few moments when his eyes were peeking in her direction. Sadly, she was hopelessly in love with him. And if she wasn't careful, she could be toxic to herself, just trying to get his attention.

She found some valiums in the medicine cabinet and decided to experiment. She thought, if she could make herself sick, Marcus would be concerned and show some compassion. She took one pill and felt a little strange: a little dizzy, just enough to want to lie down. The slight dizziness was enough to convince Shundra that two tablets would do the trick. *What? Is she crazy?* Shundra didn't want to die. She wanted to make Marcus feel her foolishness was his fault. *That's not the right or loving way to acquire compassion.*

She wanted Marcus to mend his ways and take care of the girl she felt he was destined to marry, which was her. *What? That's psychotic thinking! Who wants to knowingly marry someone who might overdose with pills or harm herself, in any way? Before the marriage even begins, she's already shown (1) her vulnerability, (2) the possibility of hurting herself severely, or maybe killing herself; then what? She still loses him! Seriously, is she that insecure?*

She manipulated Byron in finding out when Marcus would be visiting him. He told Shundra that the two of them had plans to get together on Friday, around 6:00 p.m. That was plenty of time for Shundra to plan her academy award. Her mind started working almost immediately, so she made an excuse to end the conversation with Byron. After all, she had what she wanted, and she had no extra time for the small talk. *Wow! She is becoming more scandalous than Tamara.*

Her plan seemed to have worked. On Friday, she took the first valium around 4:30 p.m. and the second one around 6:00 p.m. It was perfect timing because Marcus arrived around 6:15 p.m. The first valium had already begun to work, and she was ready for the performance of her life. She heard Marcus's car when he arrived, so the grand opening was about to begin.

Her mental capacity was slower than usual because of the valiums, so her deception was now her reality. She was a little disoriented as she slowly walked across the street. She was barely able to say hello but managed to stand with dignity. Byron spoke to her first.

"Hey, Shundra," he said with a smile on his face. Byron wasn't surprised to see Shundra, especially since he knew she was aware of Marcus's visit.

But Byron's brother interrupted their conversation because Byron had a phone call, so Marcus and Shundra were alone for a while. "Y'all, I will be back in a few minutes," said Byron.

"Hey, lady, said Marcus. 'What's going on?'

"Not mu-mu-mu-much, Shundra said.

"Why are you talking like that? asked Marcus.

"Talking like w-w-w-what? Shundra asked.

"All tongue-tied, like you have been smoking weed, said Marcus, with laughter in his voice.

"That's not f-f-f-funny. 'You know I don't smoke weed, Ma-Ma-Ma-Marcus,' she said.

"Well, what's wrong with you? he asked again.

"I took some pills, and now I d-d-d don't feel well. I didn't know I would feel like t-t-t this. Ma-Ma-Ma-Marcus, I feel like I'm going to pass out,' she said. And, she fainted, falling right into Marcus's arms.

They were leaning against the car, so Marcus held her tight with one hand and patted her face with the other to see if she responded. "Shundra, what did you take? 'Shundra, what did you take?' he said in a loud voice.

She wasn't entirely out of it because she mumbled the word "Valiums.

"How many? Marcus asked.

"Two or three, said Shundra. 'I need to lay down. I'm fine.

Marcus slowly walked Shundra home and helped her lay on the sofa. Her parents weren't there, so Marcus sat with her and watched over her while she slept. When she started snoring like someone in a good, deep sleep, Marcus felt she wasn't in any danger, so he left.

Early Saturday morning, he called to make sure Shundra was doing fine. "Good morning, sleepyhead. 'Do you feel better today?' he asked.

"I'm a little tired, she said. 'But I do feel better.'

"Shundra, I was so scared last night. Girl, I wouldn't know what to do without you. Don't ever do that again! he said. *That's what she wanted to hear!*

Marcus was expressing concern, but Shundra's ears heard love.

"Why did you take the valiums? he asked.

"Because I don't want to be without you, Marcus. Nowadays, everything is about Tamara, not about us anymore. I had a weak moment and made a bad decision. I don't want to die. I want us to be together again," she said.

Marcus didn't say a word. He can hear the tears in Shundra's voice. He knew she was hurting inside and he didn't want to give her a reason to take any more Valiums.

He felt terrible and started calling and seeing Shundra more often than before. *Maybe he is trying to do the right thing. But, how long will it last, especially since he wants Tamara, not Shundra?*

Kenneth wasn't coming around as much. *Guess all that talk about Shundra being worth the fight is beginning to take a toll.*

He still didn't know who was responsible for cutting his tires. But, he had a plan and was determined to catch the scum one way or the other.

Shundra thought she and Marcus were getting back together, so she wasn't upset that Kenneth wasn't coming by as often. However, Marcus's heart wasn't with Shundra anymore, so what Shundra thought she had with Marcus didn't last very long at all.

14

Girl Talk

It had been three weeks since Shundra and Gayle started dance class. It was Wednesday again, and Shundra needed to finish her work early so she could attend the class. As she was preparing for the night, she decided to call Gayle before leaving the job. "Do you want to get some wings from the Wing Stop by DEC before class today? Shundra asked.

"Yes, that would be great! 'I didn't have lunch today, so I will be hungry around that time,' said Gayle.

"OK, let's meet there at 6:30 p.m., said Shundra.

"OK, see you soon, said Gayle. She was excited about their meeting before class started. She felt it was an excellent opportunity to share what was happening in her life.

When Shundra arrived, Gayle was talking with one of the guys from the class. He was the tall, dark, bold, and handsome-looking guy that seemed to be acquainted with all the instructors, and of course, Gayle's prince charming. *Something is different about Gayle. She looks happy, almost glowing,* so when the guy left, Shundra said to Gayle, "Ok, girl! Spill it! 'What's going on with you two?' Gayle was laughing so hard that Shundra thought she was going to fall off the chair.

"Was it that obvious? she asked. Shundra gave her that look as if to say *you are about to fall off that chair, and you have the nerve to ask me that question.* Gayle knew what that look meant. So she proceeded with "I meant to tell you all about it, but after the open floor session, you rush out so fast like there is a fire or something, that we never get the chance to talk. Shundra gave her that look again as if to say *you got my undivided attention now, and I'm waiting.*

"Well, every Monday and Wednesday night, instead of going home, I meet Clarence at his house for dinner. During my first visit, he cooked pork chops, rosemary potatoes, and asparagus. The pork chops were ready and coming out of the oven when I arrived. Everything else was ready, so he asked me to make the Kool-Aid. Gayle laughed. 'What 50-plus man do you know still drink Kool-Aid?' she asked. Anyways, I made the Kool-Aid, and we sat down for dinner.

"To my surprise, the food was delicious. Clarence's cooking was better than some women. He took his fork and fed me every bite as if I was a baby who didn't know how to feed myself. And, girl, I did the same for him...such a romantic gesture! Then, we laid on the sofa and watched a movie. Image that: dancing the night away at DEC, eating dinner afterward, and now watching a movie together. I found it sweet and relaxing.

"Then, he made sure the night wasn't over without any playtime. He chased me around the house, trying to get my clothes off, with no success on the first night! Gayle quickly added. We were acting like little kids, and I was enjoying it, she said while grinning generously. It was fun, but I am too old for running around the house, jumping over tables, and playing 'hiding go get it.'

It was a workout, not to mention the dancing at DEC, which was enough exercise on its own for one night. It took us a minute to catch our breath after all that running around.

During the second visit, he told me I could no longer lay on his sofa or in his bed in my clothes. That was one of his dating rules. But, I didn't pay him any attention because I was enjoying the chase, and I wanted him to work for this goodness! Girl, I wasn't about to give it up that quick."

"Gayle, who are you trying to fool? Shundra asked. I know you too well. It was probably like giving a baby some candy the second time you were at his house, especially if you wanted it as bad as he did.

"Whatever, Shundra, Gayle said. "He still had to work for it. And, I must admit like Tony the tiger said, It was grrrrrreat!"

They laughed, finished their wings, went to class and enjoyed the night.

15

Club 1000

Shundra finished her weekly reports, which took at least an hour or two to complete. She ran the Total AR, the AR by Team by Employee Detail, the AR by Team by Employee Summary, the Top Employee AR Balances, the Top Customer AR Balances, the Write-Offs, the Cash Receipts, the Month End AR Aging, and the Monthly Production Reports. Afterward, she handed the reports to her manager, then left for her dance class.

The traffic was minimal, so she made it to class 15 minutes before it started. Gayle and Shundra pulled into the parking lot at the same time. Gayle wanted to share some information with her, so she was pleased to see that Shundra was not late. "Hey, Girl! I'm glad you made it on time, Gayle said. I got something I want to run by you.

"Oh, ok, what is it? asked Shundra.

"There's another dance class on Tuesday nights that's only five minutes away. I've heard nothing but good things about this place and the dance instructor. Let's check it out, said Gayle. They talked about it for a few minutes, and although Shundra was tired from the two nights a week already on her schedule, she agreed to meet Gayle there the following week.

"How's the book coming along? Gayle asked.

"Girl, I'm glad you asked. The adrenaline is pumping. It's like a sudden burst of energy controlling my fingers, typing faster than I can think. It's surprising how much I accomplish in an hour. I love it. The brain is so amazing while processing so much information. I never thought I would enjoy writing so much. Do you think it's my calling? Shundra asked.

"You'll know if an agent finds you or if someone offers you a movie deal, said Gayle, trying to be encouraging. Until then, keep writing. Time will tell soon enough! See you during the open floor session, said Gayle.

"OK, see you later," said Shundra.

There appeared to be a different crowd in class, adding new possibilities to the group. The crowd was lovely as usual, but all eyes were on the open floor session searching for an opportunity for Mr. or Miss Right with the newbies, including Shundra.

Shundra enjoyed dancing with different guys because each of them had a different technique. The instructor taught the basics, and the guys always tried to add their special moves to the dance. It's interesting sometimes, and other times, Shundra wished the guys would stick with the basics until they learn the advanced moves. But, tonight was a good night, and Shundra kept up with all the guys while dancing. However, she was tired and decided to leave early for the night, especially since no real possibilities were in her sight.

Shundra saw Clarence as he was heading toward the door and glanced over at Gayle. She knew it wouldn't be long before Gayle was leaving too. *Another chase around the house, no doubt!* As expected, Gayle made her way to Shundra and said, "Girl, it's time to play' hiding go get it!' They laugh, and since it was game time for Gayle, she said, "See you later, alligator.

Shundra replied, "I'm leaving too. After while crocodile, ENJOY!"

They smiled and went their separate ways. Gayle was out of the door before Shundra could turn around.

The following Tuesday, Gayle confirmed their plans to meet at the new dance class. It wouldn't surprise Gayle if Shundra changed her mind. Shundra sometimes said 'yes, I will go,' then found an excuse to do something different, especially if she didn't seem interested in the first place. Shundra agreed to go, for Gayle's sake only, and Gayle knew this.

The phone rung at 5:00 p.m. "Hey, Shundra. Are we still meeting tonight at Club 1000? Gayle asked.

"Yes, said Shundra. I'll be there at 7:30 p.m. "OK, but don't be late, said Gayle. We need good seats to see what's going on, just in case we want to come back.

"Yea, right, said Shundra.

"Seriously, I want to see who is coming and going, who is with whom, and all the good-looking single men when they walk in.

"Are you going to dance or to flirt? Shundra asked.

"A little of both, said Gayle.

"And, what about Clarence? Shundra asked.

"Girl, what about him? You know that's my sweetie! I am unavailable tonight, not blind! Besides, I need to keep 'my rap tight,' so I know that I still got it, Gayle said. You know how these guys are: with you one day and with someone else the next day. I don't have time for games. If Clarence starts acting up, you better believe, I am confident enough to know I can get someone else too. Anyways, I'm looking out for you as well, said Gayle.

72

"Whatever! Shundra said. Bye. I'll see you there!"

Shundra made it on time. However, the dance class was scheduled to start at 8:00 p.m. but the instructor was 45 minutes late. So, there was plenty of time to check out the club. The atmosphere was a little different from DEC: smaller, and the crowd wasn't as friendly.

Everyone appeared to be sitting with their circle of friends. DEC's group was from all over the metropolis, and they enjoyed mixing and mingling. Here, at Club 1000, it was more white-collar workers, age 30 years and up, and blue-collar and pink-collar workers, starting at age 20. It was not the crowd for ages 50-plus. But, that didn't matter to Shundra because she was only there for the dance lesson, unlike Gayle.

When the instructor finally made it, he arranged the tables and chairs accordingly. Then, he called all beginners to the floor. As usual, more women than men were in the club. The instructor invited all the men to the dance floor, regardless of their status: beginners, intermediate, or advanced dancers.

The instructor stood in the middle of the crowd and demonstrated the necessary steps: transition, full turn, half turn, walk with it, behind the back, and take it home. It was a different kind of swing-out; old-school, you might say.

Shundra didn't like the terminology. In her opinion, DEC's language was more stimulating: basic steps, he turns, she turns, behind the back, and stationary reverse.

After a few times doing the steps along with the women, the instructor showed the guys their part. He explained how to use signals as they guided the ladies into each move. Then, he told them to do it together as he watched to see if everyone understood and could make the steps as demonstrated.

Shundra's partner was annoying because he was explaining something different from the instructor. He was an advanced student, acting like he knew more than the instructor. She asked the instructor to demonstrate the moves again. She was embarrassed because everyone knew the steps, except her. She couldn't hear or pay attention to what he was saying since her partner was so annoying.

She didn't mind dancing with the advanced guys during the open floor session. She was open-minded and willing to learn new steps. But, she wanted to hear the instructions given by the instructor when he was speaking.

The instructor said, "Guys, rotate to the left," and Shundra was happy that her partner moved on to the next girl. But, her next partner's comments concerning another lady on the dance floor deeply disturbed her. "I bumped into that fat lady standing there. I hope she's not pregnant," he said. Shundra didn't respond to him, but she looked closely at him and thought to herself, *This dwarf with his old-fashioned gold tooth's got some nerve!*

Then, she walked away. *"That is something he should keep to himself,"* she thought out loud. After all, this was about dancing and having fun. She didn't come here to talk about other people with him; maybe with Gayle, but certainly not with him. Shundra was shaking her head and thinking, *This is not the place for me!*

Gayle and Shundra did not stay for the open floor session. Gayle was optimistic, but Shundra wasn't impressed with Club 1000. She enjoyed the teachings and the scheduled dates at DEC more.

Nonetheless, if Gayle wanted to go back, she would go because that's what friends do: have one another's back, even when they disagree.

16

His Voice Made Her Body Behave

Shundra had a busy day at work, starting with an 8:00 a.m. team-building meeting that lasted until noon. At 3:00 p.m., she was scheduled to meet with her manager to discuss the production changes that were about to take place. But, her focus wasn't on work. Instead, her mind continued to reflect on what to write next for her book. She couldn't miss the meeting or be late. It was now 12:30 p.m., and with the little time she had, she rushed to her car and began to type.

Tuesday - Lunch at 12:30 p.m.

Marcus started his disappearing act once again leaving Shundra with more reasons to set her radar on Kenneth. She still needed a date for the prom, so she was being sweeter than honey, and purposely accommodating Kenneth on their dates.

Kenneth was no longer worried about his car. He organized a plan of action to discourage anyone who attempted to cut his tires again. His cousins and some of his cousins' friends were cruising the neighborhood, paying close attention to the street Shundra lived on for anything that looked suspicious. Some of the crew members were felons and looking for something exciting to do. They welcomed the idea of trouble.

If Marcus was caught hanging around Kenneth's car, he was probably going to get that ass-whipping he escaped before. Shundra was not going to pretend she didn't know what was happening to save Marcus this time. The look of devastation would be her only option, which would be the perfect time to repeat Marcus's words when she showed up at Tamara's house: "What are you doing here? These people don't play! You don't want to mess with them!"

But, fortunately for Marcus and Shundra, Kenneth's cousins and friends didn't see anyone lurking around his car.

Kenneth and Shundra were much closer now that they were spending more time together. Kenneth was different from Marcus because he consistently tried to persuade her into having sex with him, and Shundra liked the chase. She knew if she waited longer, he would want her that much more and work even harder to get her.

Although she tried not to put herself in any compromising situations, it was sometimes unavoidable because Kenneth was older and more advanced. He knew how to maneuver a girl into the bedroom, and Shundra was no exception.

He said to her in a calm, soft but deep voice, "Your beauty captivates me with that Indian-looking nose that curves upward when you smile." While caressing her face with the back of his hand, he continued with, "girl, you are sexy. If I didn't know any better, I would think you were half-Indian and half-Frenchman. You have a beautiful complexion. And you smell good too."

Lying across the bed, fully dressed, slowly he stuck his wet tongue in her ear and softly blew warm and cold air from his breath. He complimented her big, pretty legs and told her to wrap them around his waist and squeeze like she's hugging him tightly. When she didn't respond to his request, he guided her legs into position. Then, he whispered, "Squeeze, baby." His voice alone was enough for her body to behave.

Kenneth said nothing of Shundra's body temperature, but she felt moderately warm. It wouldn't take much for him to get her out of those clothes, but he loved foreplay, so he took his time. "I love touching you, he said. 'I bet your body fluids are good too. Can I taste you?' he whispered. Shundra melted instantly. The sensation was so intense that she thought she would lose control. His hands were busy massaging her clothed boobs, and her nipples were busy reacting to his touch, just like the erection of his crotch.

He kissed her lips and whispered again, "Can I taste you? Baby!" Kenneth's words were hypnotizing for a moment, but suddenly the spell broke. *Aww, hell, there she goes again. Just when things are getting good!* She thinks to herself, *Can you taste me? Is he talking about the saliva from my mouth when we kissed? Marcus never said anything about tasting me.* Somehow, the thoughts of Marcus show up again at the most inconvenient time ever. It seemed Shundra could not escape her feelings of Marcus, no matter what she did. *Seriously? The dude is laying it on thick, and she's worried about what Marcus did.*

She wiggled from underneath Kenneth, and said, "It's getting late, I should go." *No, she didn't! Well, I'll be damned,* he probably thought. With the look he gave Shundra, she wondered if he was going to slap her. But instead, he respected her wishes and prepared himself to take her home.

Kenneth had a reputation to uphold. He was a smooth talker. There was no way he would let Shundra be the one who got away. Losing was not in his vocabulary. He would most definitely try again later.

Truthfully, the thought of Marcus spoiled the moment for Shundra, but she was more afraid of disappointing Kenneth than anything else due to her lack of experience like it did with Marcus.

Without Kenneth's coaching, Shundra wouldn't have known what to do. She's hooked on his voice alone, and she wanted to start over, not go home. But, Kenneth took her home and ended the night with a kiss on the cheek. "Goodnight, I will call you tomorrow, he said. *Dammit! What was I thinking?*

"Goodnight," she said sadly.

She couldn't get Kenneth's words, or his touch, or his wet tongue in her ear out of her mind. She tossed and turned the whole night. When daylight came, she was happy to get a cold shower to release her mind from "Can I taste you?" and from wondering how him tasting her would feel.

17

Date Night

Shundra was exhausted by the time she got to work. Being out two nights in a row was more than she could handle. Not to mention, today was Wednesday, and she would be doing the same thing again tonight at DEC. It crossed her mind not to attend class, but tonight, she might move to the advanced level, and she didn't want to miss out on the opportunity.

She decided to journal, maybe for 30 minutes, then use the other 30 minutes for a short nap.

Wednesday - Lunch at 2:45 p.m.

Her phone rings, so she checked to see who was calling. And, to her surprise, it was Kenneth. "Well, hello beautiful, he said, with his smooth and deep voice. Suddenly, she was overwhelmed with joy. 'Will you have dinner with me tonight?' he asked.

Shundra grinned. "Let me check my schedule for any conflicts, and if so, I will change them just for you, she said, as if she had something better to do.

"Ok, you do that, and I will pick you up tonight at 8:15 p.m. And Shundra, be ready! The reservation is at 9:00 p.m.

"Where are we going?

"Do you remember the Disney movie, *Lady and the Tramp*?

"Of course, that's one of my all-time favorites, she said.

"We're going to be Lady and the Tramp tonight at the Michelangelo Italian Restaurant.

Shundra grinned again. "Sounds like fun."

Shortly afterward, they hung up the phone, and she thought to herself, *this may be a perfect night to ask him to escort her to the prom.*

At 8:15 sharp, Kenneth was at her door with her favorite red-tipped yellow roses. He was wearing an open-collar, button-down shirt and dressy jeans. He looked stunning, Shundra thought. She was wearing a rust-colored ruffle blouse with a pair of jeans that accented every curve of her body from the waist down; Kenneth's eyes glowed with pleasure.

After dinner, they parked by a lake near the restaurant. Kenneth planted a sweet, sensual kiss behind her earlobe and followed up with more sensual kisses on her neck. It tickled, and Shundra flinched. "Do you want me to stop? Kenneth asked, with his sexy voice.

"No, don't be silly!"

He smiled and held her face with both hands as he drew her closer to plant another kiss. Shundra could feel his breath as he got closer to her face. She opened her mouth and received his luxurious tongue, and they did what came naturally.

At that very moment, Shundra knew kissing was not the only thing they would do the next time they were together. She was very curious about what he felt like inside her.

With that thought dazzling in Shundra's mind, she ended her journaling and took a quick nap. *A wet dream, no doubt!*

<u>Thursday - Lunch at 1:45 p.m.</u>

It was getting hot in the car, with all that breathing and kissing going on. Shundra didn't want to stop, but she managed to redirect her thoughts long enough to mutter, "It's getting late, we should go.

Without stopping, Kenneth whispered, "Go, where?

"Home, Shundra said.

Kenneth paused and looked at her, then he said, "Ok, I understand."

He's probably thinking, *not this again!* But, he didn't seem to be too upset.

The conversation on the way home was about the feeling they shared while being so close to one another.

Shundra was almost home when she decided to ask the question about her prom. She wasn't sure if Kenneth would accept, but he said, "It would be a pleasure to escort the most beautiful lady at the school to her prom."

Shundra was excited. The prom was two months away, and she felt relieved that her search for a prom date was over.

18

Meet Anthony Walker, Mr. Complicated

From a distance, Shundra could feel the eyes of a stranger staring her up and down, and it was annoying. It was like someone in a horror movie, unknowingly being targeted and attacked by surprise. Quickly, she searched her surroundings and saw a little, Oreo-skin-toned, silver-headed man gazing at her with the smile of approval. Their eyes met, and he smiled more, as he walked toward her direction.

"Hello, beautiful. I'm Anthony. Would you like to dance? he asked. Shundra couldn't get over the feeling that something bad was about to happen.

"No, not right now, she said. 'Maybe, later.' Honestly, he didn't seem to be her type.

"Maybe in 10 or 15 minutes? he asked.

With a smirk on her face, Shundra nodded her head in agreement, even though she wasn't impressed with the idea.

"Sure," she said.

Two seconds later, a barrel-chested, fair-complexioned, salt-and-pepper-haired man stepped toward Shundra and held out his hand, then asked, "May I have this dance?"

She smiled and thought to herself, *what a hottie!* Without hesitation, she reached for his hand, and he led her to the dance floor. Anthony, standing nearby, looked at her and nodded to acknowledge, *Oh, I see how it is!* He didn't seem disappointed, and he still had that same smile of approval on his face.

Shundra thought this was the end of Anthony, but three minutes into the dance, he walked over and asked, "May I cut in?" Mr. Hottie stepped back and let him cut in. *What a couple of jerks,* Shundra thought. *Anthony for being so bold, and Mr. Hottie for being so weak!* She didn't want to cause a scene, so she politely accepted Anthony's hand to dance.

With the triumph, Anthony grinned as they begin. "You dance well, he said.

"Thank you, she responded calmly.

"Are you dating anyone?

"Yes, I am, she said.

"Really? Where is he? Why isn't he here with you? Anthony asked. Shundra was thinking, *why can't he dance and keep his mouth shut? He's lucky I'm dancing with him.*

Anthony could sense how uneasy Shundra was with his questions, so before she responded, he said, 'If you were mine, I wouldn't trust these guys around you. You are breathtaking! Pretty lady, I mean that as a compliment.'

"Well, thank you, Anthony, she said. 'Do it change things, knowing I am dating someone?' Shundra asked.

"No. I'm not worried about your man. He should be here with you, Anthony genuinely replied.

"My thoughts exactly!" she responded with a bigger grin on her face. Shundra was thinking, *this man may not be my type, but what he said certainly made sense.*

Shundra had a long-distance boyfriend, but he wasn't around long enough to make a difference, which was why the door of opportunity was open. She didn't talk much about him, not even to Gayle, because she no longer considered him as a boyfriend. The two of them act more like friends who visited one another occasionally than two people in a serious relationship. So, Anthony talked his way into Shundra's world with a simple honest of opinion. *Mission accomplished!* he thought silently.

It was nice for a while. After leaving DEC, on some occasions, Shundra followed Anthony to his place of business, which was also where he resided and where they practiced the dance moves previously learned. During these visits, Shundra saw Anthony as a very passionate person. But, later on, she discovered he was also possessive.

She learned of his medical issue: he had diabetes and required insulin. She didn't like needles, and she wasn't sure if she could be around someone who needed injections once or twice a day. But, Anthony was a pro at administering the doses to himself. So, Shundra was fine as long as she didn't have to see it done.

Besides, she enjoyed the wake-up calls. "Wake up, happy feet," he said around 7:00 a.m. every morning. And, every Friday night, for date night, after he closed the shop, they went to The Movie Grill for dinner and a movie. Before leaving his shop, gently he cupped her face and planted a big, mushy kiss on her lips, and another one when the movie was over.

It was the little things he did that warmed her heart, like the gift and the presentation of the intimacy desired. Anthony stared directly into her eyes and gave her a bag filled with black-and-white tissue. She opened the bag and was surprised to see a black, vibrating gorilla, making grunting sounds.

"It's cute, she said, with a strange look on her face.

"Girl, do you know what that means? Anthony asked.

Shundra was perplexed. *It's a stuffed animal that vibrates*, she thought. Anthony clearly understood that Shundra had no idea of what he was suggesting.

He said, "Girl, that's a gorilla in heat. Gorillas vibrate and make that grunting sound when they want to mate! 'I want to mate with you!' he said with a glow in his eyes and a big grin on his face.

Shundra burst into a loud laugh. Anthony was serious as a heart attack, and Shundra thought it was funny. The smile dropped from his face, the room was quiet, and the romantic gesture was over.

Unfortunately, other things begin to end as well, like her enjoying dancing at DEC. Shundra couldn't stop looking over her shoulder because Anthony didn't like her dancing with other guys. She felt like a criminal who was afraid her past would catch up with her.

She didn't realize Anthony's possessiveness until she invited him to her sister's friend's birthday party. Shundra was dancing and having a wonderful time when Anthony confronted her after she finished dancing with a guy who was teaching her how to two-step.

"Let's go, he said after Shundra returned to her seat.

"Why? Shundra asked.

Anthony didn't hide his feelings. "You are dancing with other guys, and I don't like it. I am your man, and I will not have you disrespect me. I'm ready to go.

"We danced. That's all! Shundra declared.

Anthony looked nervous, tired, low on energy, and apparently not thinking clearly.

"Are you feeling well? she asked.

85

"I will be if I can find some orange juice, he said. 'Then, I'm ready to go.' Shundra did not respond. They left shortly afterward.

This behavior was a side of Anthony that she did not recognize, and she was beginning to see it too often, especially while at DEC.

He stood in the center of the dance floor next to Shundra while she was dancing with someone else. Shundra continued to dance, but she was very uncomfortable. When the dance was over, he grabbed her arm, and while leading her towards their table, he said, "I told you I don't like it when you dance with other guys."

Again, Anthony appeared irritable and possibly hypoglycemia. With each episode, he became more embarrassing around Shundra, like emotionally abusive. She tried to be understanding because of his diabetes, but it overwhelmed her. So, she decided to end the relationship. He was very apologetic, but the mood swings were unbearable.

The next day, Shundra rung Anthony's phone several times, but he didn't answer. She started to worry and wanted to stop by his shop during her lunch break. It was an hour drive from her job to his, so instead, she took the rest of the evening off.

The front of the building was glass so that one could see inside of the central office. Anthony didn't appear to be inside. But, he spent a lot of time in the back where he resides, so Shundra continued to knock and dial his phone.

She could hear the phone ringing, so she thought something was wrong. Shundra tried not to panic. She considered calling 911 but wasn't sure that was the best thing to do. She thought, *what if he's not here?*

86

Finally, Anthony came to the door. "What are you doing here? he asked.

"Really? Shundra said. 'I'm standing here worrying about you, thinking something had happened and wondering if I could help you. And, you don't have the decency to say hello and, I'm ok.'

"Shundra, don't come here acting as if you care about me. Because if you did, you would respect me as your man when we are out in public. A grown man don't need you checking up on him!' he snarled.

"Anthony, I took off of work to come and check on you. When you didn't answer your phone, I didn't know what to think, especially since your blood sugar levels had been off lately.

"I am a grown-ass man. Shundra, I do not need you to check up on me! he exclaimed once again.

"OK, it won't happen again, Shundra replied as she walked out the door.

Her emotions were all over the place. *I don't understand this man! How can he be so stubborn, judging, criticizing, and condemning? But, so caring, and yet complicated too.*

19

Heart-to-Heart Talk

Shundra and Gayle hadn't seen one another since their visit to Club 1000. Gayle was, no doubt, enjoying her time with Clarence, but she would take the time to talk with Shundra if she called. Shundra hadn't called with anything of importance, until now.

"Gayle, its Shundra. Give me a call when you get a moment. I need to talk." Shundra's phone pings immediately. It's a text from Gayle. *I'm in a meeting. Will call afterward.* Shundra texted, *Okay.*

Finally, Gayle called. "Girl, what's going on with you? Something has to be wrong for you to call and say you need to talk.

"Well, there is, I wanted to tell you about Anthony, Shundra replied.

"Anthony? You have been holding out on me! Who the heck is Anthony? Gayle insisted.

"Someone, I met at DEC the night you and Clarence missed class, doing who knows what! Shundra said.

"Well, sounds like you been doing who knows what yourself! Gayle giggled.

"Gayle, seriously, do you think you are the only one who should

88

have some fun? Shundra laughed.

"No, but from the sound of your voice message, you weren't having much fun, Gayle said. "What's wrong?

"Anthony is like Dr. Jekyll and Mr. Hyde, said Shundra. One minute he's patient, kind, not rude or self-seeking. The man is protective and trustworthy. But, in an instant, he turns into this opinionated, judging, criticizing, condemning Grinch, Shundra explained. And, I do believe he will hurt me.

"Damn, Shundra. How is it, that all the weirdos are attractive to you, and apparently, you to them? I don't get it, said Gayle.

"I know, said Shundra. 'It's like I don't know how to pick a good man!'

"No, I don't think that's it, Gayle replied. I think you go overboard with the benefit of a doubt strategy. Everything with you is fine until given a reason that says otherwise. You should follow your intuition, Gayle said, 'and not this innocent until proven guilty strategy that you always use.' I'm sure you felt something strange about this guy when you met him, right? Gayle asked.

"I did, said Shundra, but he won me over with his perseverance and his honesty.

"Describe Anthony so that I can look for him in dance class, Gayle said.

"He's a short, Oreo-skin-toned, silver-headed man, not bad-looking at all, Shundra replied.

"What type of car does he drive? Gayle asked.

"OMG, Gayle! Why do you need to know what type of car he drives? Shundra shouts. You take everything to the extreme!

"And, you should too, Gayle said. It's called a back-up plan! It doesn't hurt to be extra careful, she said with persistence.

89

"He drives a grey Toyota Tacoma, Shundra said calmly.

"Do you know the license plate number? Gayle asked.

"You need that too? Seriously, Gayle! Do you gather all of this information on every guy you date?

"Shundra, you need to open your eyes and see what's going on in today's world. It's not 1979 anymore. If you cut in front of someone on the freeway, or flip them off, you may get shot. Good Samaritans get ran over or shot and left to fend for themselves more often than not, said Gayle, as she continued with the daily news. Nowadays, 24 hours later, after a date, your body could end up at the bottom of the lake, buried, burned, or cut into pieces. Information is necessary; it helps! And yes, I keep it all recorded in my cell phone, just in case, because you never know what will happen. If Anthony does anything that causes you harm, I want the police to find him as quick as possible, said Gayle in her warm and sensitive voice. I love you, girl!

"Alright, love you too," said Shundra.

"I got to go back to work. We'll talk later, said Gayle.

"Okay, I will call you tonight, replied Shundra. And, make sure you have all the 411 on Anthony ready for me, okay, Shundra?

"Bye, Gayle."

20

Prom Night with Kenneth

Shundra's cell phone didn't get good reception in her office all the time. So she walked to the north side of the building, a cozy little area that overlooked the interstate, when Gayle called. She didn't return to her office immediately; instead, Shundra stood there for a moment gazing out the window, thinking about the things Gayle said. Shundra needed to get back to work as well, but her thoughts weren't cooperating with the reality of the reports remaining on her desk. She decided to take an early lunch, and what better way to clear her thoughts than to spend more time writing her book. Besides, her feelings of Kenneth were more soothing right now than her thoughts of Anthony.

Friday - Lunch at 12:45 p.m.

She wore a magenta-colored, mermaid-style dress with a strapless neckline and a fishtail train, very simple, but elegant, and complimentary. When Kenneth arrived at Shundra's house for the prom, he took one look at her and said with the biggest grin on his face, "Girl, you are breathtaking! I got to be the luckiest guy at the prom tonight! Shundra was blushing and reaching for the gorgeous corsage, white roses with a magenta ribbon that Kenneth was holding.

"Thank you, she said with a huge smile.

Kenneth wore a black tuxedo with skinny lapel illusions, white shirt, and a magenta tie.

"And, you look very nice yourself, Shundra said to Kenneth with a gleam in her eyes.

"Shall we go? Kenneth asked.

"Not yet. My mom wants to take pictures first, she responded.

They spent 30 minutes posing for the camera before heading to the prom. Along the way, Kenneth continued with the compliments.

"Babe, what perfume are you wearing? he asked.

"My mom said it's J'adore. It means I love you! Do you like it? Shundra asked.

"Your mom has good taste, he said. Baby, I will be smelling you in my dreams tonight. *First, it was can I taste you? Now, he will smell me too!* Shundra thought.

"Yep, it's going to be a wet dream tonight. He laughed, then reached for her hand to hold.

Shundra wasn't sure how to respond to his remark, so she simply squeezed his hand, and laughing said, "Okay, sweet dreams!"

It was right on time because finally, they arrived at the prom. Kenneth opened the door and helped Shundra out of the car.

Shundra couldn't wait to show off her date. She spotted her friends almost immediately, and they ran towards her as soon as they saw her.

"Aww, Shundra, you look so beautiful, one of the girls said.

"Thank you, and so do you, Shundra said, before proudly introducing her date.

"Everybody, this is my date, Kenneth.

"Hello, said Kenneth. It's nice to meet you all."

They all said their hellos, then sat together at a table in the middle of the ballroom. While the servers prepared dinner: chicken, seasonal vegetables, potatoes, tea, and cheesecake, the guest speakers presented their motivational speeches. Afterward, the class president announced the prom king and queen, and the senior class was satisfied with the winners. After dinner, the music started, and the senior class mixed and mingled and danced until midnight.

Surprisingly, for the first time, the thought of Marcus did not interrupt Shundra's beautiful and enjoyable evening with her date.

Shundra was certain their last stop of the night would be at a nice hotel, especially since the two of them could hardly contain themselves on their previous date. But, Kenneth was a perfect gentleman from beginning to end. After the dance, he took Shundra home and ended the night with a gentle kiss on the lips. *What a tease!* But, from that night forward, Shundra's melting heart for Marcus was full of cool breezes and sunshine. Marcus had finally vanished entirely.

Shundra returned from lunch and saw a sticky note on her desk. It was from Deanna, asking if she wanted to have lunch at Brown's BBQ again next week. Shundra enjoyed their last luncheon and was happy that she had asked. Before starting on the reports still waiting on her desk to complete, she called Deanna and accepted her offer.

"Monday, around 1:00 p.m. works for me. Is that okay with you? Shundra asked Deanna.

"Sounds good, she said. I will meet you there."

21

Deanna Asks For Advice

Shundra was running five to ten minutes late. And, as usual, Deanna arrived on time and was sitting, patiently waiting on Shundra.

"Girl, I had a last-minute call that I had to take before leaving the office. Sorry, I'm late.

"Not a problem, Deanna says. Glad you made it. I ordered our drinks already.

"Oh, okay, thank you, said Shundra. So, what's happening on your end at work? Shundra asked.

"A lot of changes going on with hierarchy, and even more gossip with all the firing and hiring taking place, Deanna replied. But, I try not to let it bother me much because for my life, I know God is in control.

"That is certainly true. You can't put your trust in people. They will disappoint you most of the time, Shundra said with a shrug. And, on our end, the meetings and the constant changes to reports are never-ending, so it seems, but we do what we can and try not to complain.

"I agree, says Deanna. We are blessed to have jobs."

Shundra and Deanna ordered their food. And, while waiting,

Deanna decided to share a friend's horrific experience. The situation involved her friend's husband, and she knew how sensitive it was, but she also knew she could trust Shundra with the information. So, she changed the subject from life at the office to a more private matter.

"Shundra, you said if I ever needed to talk, you would be here for me. And today, I really need to talk, said Deanna.

"Sure! I meant every word. I'm here for you, Shundra replied.

"It's about my friend, Courtney, who was devastated after agreeing with her husband to do something totally out of her character. She loves her husband and wanted to work things out, but now, she isn't sure because she feels his request is disrespectful and degrading. I don't know how to help her. I thought maybe an outsider such as yourself could offer some advice. I felt so helpless, unable to convey any comforting words to help her cope with the situation.

"Deanna, I don't know what happened in this marriage, but already I am dubious of your involvement. Early advice, premature advice, or even specific advice could be more damaging than you may realize. You should listen and offer to pray with her. The ultimate decision on how to handle the situation is between her and God, Shundra advised.

"I understand that, but this deals with emotional abuse, and I am afraid she may not recover from it. She refused to see a counselor because of her embarrassment. I want to help her if I can.

"I'm not sure how I can assist you, but go ahead and tell me what happened, Shundra said.

"Ok, Deanna, replied. Keep in mind that I am paraphrasing. Her husband knew she wanted to try and make the marriage work. He took advantage of the fact, in my opinion, and she fell into a trap.

95

For many years, she could not understand why they had financial problems. Although he wasn't straightforward in the beginning, he decided to confess why he had no money. He said he was addicted to porn and that he spent a lot of money on peepholes.

What little knowledge she knew on the subject was from the Internet and adult movies. She was so naïve that he suggested exposing her to his world to help her understand his position. She didn't believe such behavior existed so close to home.

"Please don't tell me she agreed to such nonsense, Shundra said.

"Unfortunately, she did, Deanna replied, 'but that's not the worst of it.' He rode her around the area, showing her the location of the peepholes. After pointing out the third location, he moved on, then pulled into a fourth location to go inside. I guess her curiosity got the best of her because she agreed to go inside as well. She knew he was familiar with the place because when they walked in, immediately he went to the back to pay, leaving her to observe the surroundings, I assumed. I don't think she understood the expectation. She said she saw three or four women in a room, dressed in pretty negligees, playing card games.

"You mean to tell me that your friend had no idea of the type of sex activities performed in this place?

"Honestly, I don't think she did, said Deanna. When her husband returned, he wasn't alone. He was with a lady that escorted them to a small, sleazy room, with what looked like a camping cot for a bed, a chair, and a cheap-looking cabinet. Then, someone called her husband to the front desk, leaving her alone for a few minutes with this lady.

"I'm not sure I want to hear the rest, said Shundra with a disturbed shrug.

"It gets worse, Deanna said.

"The lady sensed how uneasy she appeared, sitting in the corner of the cot against the wall on the right-hand side, bent over and holding tightly to her blouse. She told her that the first time was always the hardest. She said, the wives usually don't feel comfortable until after a few visits with their husbands. My friend still had no idea what was about to happen. She did, however, think her husband wanted her to perform sex with another woman in his presence. And, if that was the case, it wasn't happening, she said.

"But, to her surprise, her husband returned to the room, the lady closed the door, and he took off his clothes. The lady took off her clothes, laid at the foot of the cot on the left-hand side, and the two of them started rubbing and touching one another. My friend was in shock. It wasn't what she expected. The lady looked at her and said, 'Join us.' Her husband insisted the same, but tears ran down her face as she curled into the fetal position, paralyzed and afraid of what would happen next. Her husband and the lady moaned and groaned with pleasure, and it wasn't long before the two of them were performing oral sex on one another, then intercourse, right in front of her.

"Oh, Deanna. I am so sorry she endured such disrespect, said Shundra.

"I know, Deanna replied. She said snot ran from her nose like a running faucet, out of control, as she gripped her blouse, moving closer and closer to the wall, unable to move her hands to wipe it away.

"When they climaxed, it was over. The lady quickly grabbed her clothes and left the two of them alone in the room. He put on his clothes, then reached to help her off the cot. Still in the fetal position, crying and holding her blouse tightly, she jerked her upper body away from him, as if to say, don't you dare touch me. She managed to say, get me out of here. I want to go home.

"She walked out of the room, still holding her blouse tightly, snot running down her face with her head hung down, feeling besmirched and ashamed. Her husband and the lady did not touch her; but still, she felt raped and stripped of her identity.

Shundra was shaking her head, feeling heartbroken for Deanna's friend. "Poor thing, Shundra said.

"My thoughts, exactly, said Deanna. My friend said when she got inside the car, she couldn't face her husband. She hugged the doorknob and prayed he wouldn't touch her or try to explain, and most of all, she hoped he had sense enough to sleep in a separate room. She couldn't mentally cope with anything else, she said.

"The following day was a family gathering. She had no idea how to hide the pain and suffering inside her heart. The excessive crying caused her eyes to swell and her tear duct to clog. She tried applying pressure with a warm washcloth to her eyes, but it didn't seem to give her much relief from the pain or the swelling. She didn't want to re-live the ordeal again by explaining to her family what happened, not to mention the embarrassment too.

"Wow, how did she handle that? Shundra asked.

"Not very well, she said. She hid in her uncle's bedroom, pretending to be sick versus heart-sick.

"For the most part, the family left her alone, but her uncle finally said, 'I know you are not sick, what happened? What did he do? I know he did something because I know that look when I see it. What happened?

"Did she tell him? Shundra asked.

"Yes, she did, said Deanna. She said it helped a little bit because she released the burden of holding it all inside.

"Good for her, Shundra said. Well, Deanna, again, I don't know how either of us can help her. Maybe she should see a counselor, Shundra suggested.

"I mentioned it to her, but I don't think she will, replied Deanna.

"You are a good friend, Deanna. Keep doing what you are doing: listening, comforting when you can, and continue to let her know whatever she needs, you are there for her. That's the best advice I can offer, said Shundra.

"Thank you, said Deanna. Honestly, this conversation helped me too. I needed to release it as well.

"I'm happy to hear it. I wish I could do more, said Shundra. It's time we head back to work, but if you need me, remember, I'm a phone call away.

"Okay, thanks again, said Deanna."

They left a tip on the table and headed back to work.

22

More Disturbing News from Deanna's Friend

Almost three months had passed since Deanna spoke with her friend Courtney. When her name appeared on her caller ID, all sorts of eerie feelings began to surface in the pit of her stomach. Instead of answering, Deanna waited for her to leave a message so she could brace herself for what was to come. "Hi, Deanna. It's Courtney. Give me a call, please. Girl, you won't believe what Joseph has done now," the message said. *What could be worse than what he has already done?* Deanna thought.

Ten minutes later, Deanna returned Courtney's call. "Hey, Courtney. I've been thinking about you a lot lately. I intended to call you last week but got so busy at work and never found the right time to call. But, I've been praying for you. Are you okay?

"Yes, I'm fine, taking it one day at a time, said Courtney. I called to let you know that Joseph decided he wanted a divorce, so he moved out. But to my surprise, he is doing well with making sure the kids and I have what we need to move forward.

"Well, that's good news, said Deanna.

"Wait, you haven't heard the whole story yet, replied Courtney.

Instantly, the eerie feeling surfaced once again in the pit of Deanna's stomach. Then, she remembered Shundra's advice: keep doing what you are doing; listening, comforting when you can, and continue to let her know whatever she needs, you are there for her.

Courtney continued, saying, "It seems since he left, my car has given me all sorts of problems. Joseph offered to have his mechanic check it out, so he came by the house, and supposedly, took the car to his friend. He gave me some lame excuse and said he paid the guy to fix the problem. I tried not to overthink it because, in my opinion, that was the least he could do. After all, I still had the responsibility of getting the kids to and from their everyday activities. I thanked him, and he left. No big deal, right? Courtney asked, and immediately answered the question. 'WRONG,' she said. Let me just say, God is awesome! He knew what he was doing when he gave every woman intuition. Now, if we can only learn to use it properly, maybe we can avoid a lot of unnecessary issues, she said.

I was beginning to think something was wrong with me, said Courtney. On several occasions, I felt like someone was inside my house. It was the little things that seemed to be out of place like maybe the barstools weren't as close to the bar as I usually keep them. Or, perhaps the mail I left on the bar was in a slightly different order than the way I recalled leaving it. I realize now that I was ignoring the intuition God gave us to use for our protection.

"Well, that's understandable, said Deanna. I'm not sure if any of us would have overthought the barstool or the mail.

"Well, the tables quickly turned when I stumbled on the tape recorder found underneath my car seat. I knew then that the barstool and the mail were not part of my imagination. While listening to the recorder, I realized it was approximately two weeks of my conversations on the cell phone. And it was two weeks ago that Joseph supposedly took my car to his friend for repairs. I experienced an epiphany right away: Joseph fixed my car only to record my conversations. And if he had a recorder in my car, he certainly had recorders in the house as well. Being friendly and coming by to check on the kids was his way of verifying what was on the recorders, making sure they weren't full.

"Do he think you have someone else? Deanna asked.

"I don't think so, said Courtney. Since he is planning a divorce, I think he is trying to find a way to prove I am an unfit mother so he can get the kids, she said.

"Seriously? Deanna said. Joseph knows you are a good mother.

"Yeah, but good people are accused of things they didn't do all the time, Courtney replied. Planting the benefit of the doubt is all he needed to do. And, Joseph was probably trying to find something to use in his favor.

"Did you find the recorders inside the house? Deanna asked.

"Not at first, but I did purposely arrange the mail a certain way and paid close attention to the days I expected Joseph to stop by. And, sure enough, he tampered with the mail. Afterward, I decided to get the locks changed, and once again, discovered the windows in the kid's bedroom, my bedroom, and the den area was not locked. That's how he was getting inside the house all this time—through the windows!

Sometime after that happened, my whirlpool bathtub was clogged. The plumber knocked over a plant I had sitting next to the window. Surprise! The recorder fell out of the pot. I searched the house and found another recorder under the pillow of the sofa, in the den.

Eventually, Joseph slipped up, and I caught him in the act, searching for his handiwork. I told him, 'Don't bother looking for the recorders. I found all of them.' The look on his face was worth the humiliation, Courtney said.

Deanna could hear the delight in her voice. "My friend, you have gone through a lot with this man, said Deanna.

"I know, said Courtney. I am so ready for a change. "Hang in there, Deanna said, trying to be encouraging. You are a good-hearted person, and I believe your time for a change is coming sooner than you think.

"Thank you, Deanna.

"I know you have to get back to work, so I will let you go, but keep in touch, okay? Courtney said.

"I will, Deanna responded. And you call me if you need me, okay?

"Okay, we'll talk later. Goodbye," said Courtney.

23

A Bittersweet Moment

It's Wednesday, and Shundra wasn't sure if she wanted to attend dance class tonight or not. Anthony was unstable sometimes, and Shundra wasn't sure how to react if he was around. *Should I ignore him or act as if nothing happened?* she thought to herself, with a little anxiety. Then, Gayle called. "Hey, Shundra, just checking to see if you are going to class tonight.

"The thought crossed my mind before you called, Shundra answered.

"Well, are you going? Gayle urgently asked again.

"I'm not sure, said Shundra.

"Shundra, it's a simple yes or no question! Why the hesitation? Gayle asked.

"Gayle, what if Anthony is there tonight? Shundra said with sadness in her voice.

"OMG! Shundra, you cannot let this man dictate your life! So what if he's there? You don't owe him anything! You don't have to dance with him! You don't even have to speak to him! Just come tonight, dance, and enjoy yourself! Clarence and I are going. I promise we will keep a close eye on you!

"Better yet, we can meet in the parking lot, so we all walk in together. And, if it makes you feel better, we can leave together tonight as well.

"OK, that sounds good, said Shundra. I'll be there at 7:00 p.m., no later than 7:05 p.m."

Shundra arrived at DEC at 7:05 p.m. and the three of them walked inside together.

Shundra and Gayle strolled the place to see if Anthony was there, and Clarence looked for an available table for three. They didn't find Anthony, but it was still early, and possible that he would show up. Until then, they plan to enjoy themselves without looking over their shoulders.

Shundra was sitting at the table alone while Gayle and Clarence were on the dance floor. Suddenly, she hears, "Would you like to dance?" She was astonished as she looked up and saw a distinguished-looking man smiling and waiting to hear, yes as her reply. Shundra couldn't imagine saying no to such a great, chestnut-chocolate skin tone, with a touch of salt-and-pepper hair, enticing, charming, and yummy-looking guy. "Sure," she said, grinning from ear to ear.

He began the dance moves with a start off, then an elegant spin of he turns, she turns, spinning Shundra right into his arms. Gayle's eyes were on Shundra, making sure Anthony wasn't the one dancing with her. She gave Shundra the thumbs up, and Shundra nodded her head to let her know all was good.

Shundra and Mr. Distinguished danced three more songs before leaving the dance floor. He kindly escorted Shundra to her seat, and like the gentleman he appeared to be, he pulled out the chair for Shundra, then asked, "Do you mind me sitting with you?

"No, Shundra said with pleasure.

"I'm Edmond Johnston and your name? he asked.

"Shundra," she replied.

"Nice to meet you, Shundra, he said. I hope you don't mind me asking, but are you involved with anyone?

Immediately, Shundra's thoughts turned to Anthony. "Is that a yes or no? Edmond asked.

"Is what, a yes or no? Shundra retorted.

"That, 'I'm not sure expression on your face,' he replied.

Shundra smiled and said, "Oh, I'm sure I'm not involved with anyone, but I'm not sure if my ex feels the same way. He's very possessive and doesn't always take no for an answer.

"Is he here? Edmond asked.

"I certainly hope not, Shundra said. But, I did meet him here, and there's a great possibility that he will be here. Is that a problem? Shundra asked.

"Not for me, said Edmond. And it shouldn't be a problem for you either if things are over between the two of you.

Shundra agreed.

"Do you come here often? Shundra asked Edmond.

"No, this is my second time at DEC, but my first visit left an intense craving to return, and I'm glad I did since I met you tonight.

"I'm glad you did too, said Shundra. So, what do you do for a living, if you don't mind me asking?

"I work as a media spokesman for a large company, Edmond replied.

"Interesting, Shundra said. You must have an excellent reputation with the company. You certainly dress to par and have a fantastic personality.

"Thank you for noticing. I try my best every day, said Edmond. So, what do you do for a living, if you don't mind me asking? Edmond said with a grin on his face.

"Don't mind at all. I work for a recruiting firm, in the accounting department, Shundra replied.

"Nice, Edmond responded, then asked, May I get your phone number?

"Sure, Shundra said without a second thought.

They exchanged phone numbers, then Edmond asked,

"Would you like to dance again?

"Yes, I would, Shundra said while reaching for his hand to lead the way."

Two minutes into the second song, the voice Shundra dreaded to hear boldly spoke, "Say, man, may I cut in?" Shundra isn't surprised that it's Anthony, but she was disappointed. *Please, God, let Edmond say no!*

"As a matter of fact, I do, said Edmond. I'm enjoying this lovely lady. *Thank you, Lord! Someone who's not afraid to stand up to this man!* If looks could kill, both Edmond and Shundra were as good as dead. But, it was a bittersweet moment for Shundra.

Edmond and Shundra continued dancing while Anthony took a seat and tried to intimidate them both by staring. When that didn't work, Anthony decided to dance purposely next to Shundra, attempting to make her jealous. But, Edmond had all of Shundra's attention, so Anthony's tricks spectacularly backfire. *Another bittersweet moment!*

Edmond and Shundra made their way back to their seats. Clarence and Gayle were sitting, so Shundra introduced them to Edmond. While Clarence and Edmond were talking, Gayle whispered to Shundra, "I saw your rude friend, Anthony.

"Yeah, and my new friend, Edmond, handled him well! I think he's a keeper, Shundra proudly replied.

"Maybe, but take your time, girl. Don't rush into anything right now, said Gayle. Anthony had that strange look on his face. Who knows what he might try!"

Edmond interrupted their conversation, "Is your friend going to be a problem? he asked.

"I'm not sure of what he may or may not do. Anthony is unstable, Shundra explained again.

"Will you be all right? he asked.

"I think so, and thanks for the concern, she responded.

"Not a problem, Edmond said. I don't like disrespectful guys. If there's anything I can do to help, let me know. Sometimes, guys like that need to know man to man who has a lady's back, and sweetheart, I got your back.

"That's nice of you, Shundra said. But, you don't know me that well. We just met tonight.

"True, Edmond said. But, I can tell the type of lady you are by the way you carry yourself, and I want to get to know you better. I can't have you wondering about some dude in your past, while I'm trying to show you a better future.

Shundra was speechless for a moment. *Is this guy pulling my leg or what?* "I guess time will tell what the future holds," she said mischievously.

"Shundra, it's getting late. Clarence and I are getting ready to leave. Are you prepared to go? Gayle asked. We don't want to leave you here alone, knowing Anthony is still here.

"Ok, Shundra said. It is getting late, and we both have to go to work in the morning. I will leave with you guys.

"It was nice meeting you, Shundra said to Edmond.

"Same here, Edmond replied. I will walk you to your car." The four of them passed Anthony as they were walking out; he seemed disturbed, even though he was on the floor dancing with some girl. He paused, while cautiously watching Shundra, seeing who was with her as she walked out the door.

Edmond opened the car door for Shundra, and as she was getting inside, she looked toward the entrance of DEC and saw Anthony lurking around, eyeballing her every move.

"How long does it take you to get home? Edmond asked.

"Not that long, maybe twenty minutes, Shundra said.

"Ok, call me, and let me know you made it home safely. Will you do that for me, Shundra? Edmond asked.

"Yes, I will, Shundra replied.

Ten minutes later, Shundra's phone rings. It's Anthony. She ignored the first call, but Anthony hung up and called again and again. It was annoying, so finally, on the fifth call, she answered.

"Hello, she said.

"So, that's the new guy, Anthony rudely asked.

"What do you want, Anthony? Shundra said.

"I want to know if that's your new man, he responded.

"Bye, Anthony! I don't owe you anything, and I don't have to answer your questions. Please stop calling me!

"Well, I guess that's a yes, he said, answering the question himself.

Shundra hung up before any more insults. But, it seemed that Anthony was hitting redial because Shundra's phone rung almost immediately, still she didn't answer.

Shundra quickly pulled into her garage, hoping Anthony did not follow her home. The phone stopped ringing, so she felt safe, for the moment. She settled in for the night before calling Edmond.

"Hi, it's Shundra, letting you know that I made it home safely.

"Hello, Shundra. I'm glad you made it. Any problems with your ex? Edmond asked.

"No, not at all, she said.

"Just what I wanted to hear. Thanks for calling me. You have a good night and sweet dreams, he responded.

"You too, she said.

Edmond replied, "I'm sure I will, beaming inside with joy."

24

Edmond Passes the Red Flags

Shundra didn't want to waste any of her precious time dating guys who weren't interested in a committed relationship. And she certainly didn't want to spend another second with anyone else like Anthony. Relationships begin with communication. It is the first thing Shundra scrutinizes when she first meets a guy, especially after experiencing a conversation such as this: "Hi, it's Shundra." After saying hello, the guy said nothing for a few seconds. In a moment of awkwardness, Shundra asked, "Did I catch you at a bad time?

"No, he said. Why would you ask that? I answered the phone, so obviously, I can talk. Shundra was thinking, *what kind of first response is this?*

He continued with, 'you are assuming, and the one thing I do not like is assuming.'

Shundra attempted to explain, "Well, you are holding the phone with nothing to say, and you sound like maybe this isn't a good time for you to talk.

"OK, let's do this, the guy said. Let's start over. You don't assume anything from me, and I won't assume anything from you."

His attitude was an instant red flag for Shundra and most definitely a deal-breaker! She only asked the question to avoid assuming what was going on. Clearly, this relationship wasn't going anywhere because there were communication problems from the very beginning.

Resolving conflict is another compelling red flag for Shundra. A man must have a real understanding of forgiveness—knowing it is not for the other person, but oneself. In understanding this reality, conflicts sometimes aren't quickly resolved, but one can agree to disagree and come to some form of mutual acceptance and move forward.

You can learn a lot by listening to a man who talks about his past relationships. Shundra recalled meeting a guy who had not seen or spoken with his kids in over thirty years. His kids were adults with children of their own. She tried her darnedest to get him to reach out and connect with his flesh and blood, but he refused. The only reasonable excuse not to do so, in his mind, was problems with the ex-wife. Mentally, Shundra could not fathom such a justification. She thought it was more than that—he was afraid and didn't know how to connect with his kids. Regardless, conflicts from thirty years ago shouldn't stop a man from trying to reunite with his children. Shundra didn't know all the details, but she felt that any disputes in their relationship would only lead to its end due to his unwillingness. This logic that was manifesting in Shundra's heart, he never understood. His kids are his blood; if he didn't do it for them, he certainly wouldn't do it for her. And, that's exactly how it was, unwillingness to address their problems, and so the relationship ended. From that day forward, Shundra understood the importance of two people in a relationship learning how to resolve conflict: it is a requirement, not an amenity.

Cheating (a man trying to get with a woman while married, living with, or dating someone else) is the ultimate red flag for Shundra. Under no circumstances is it acceptable! Shundra was livid when a guy she had known for a couple of weeks said to her, "Hey, babe, I got a new cell phone number. You can call me on this one because the other one, I mainly use it for work."

Immediately, Shundra recognized this action as "game," the oldest trick in the book and a huge red flag!

This guy called her promptly at the same time every night, while supposedly on his way home from work. According to him, he worked late nights. *How convenient,* Shundra thought. Outside the midnight hours, he wasn't available to take her calls. His explanation was either he didn't hear the phone ring, or he was asleep.

Soon, the misconception and the darkness all turned to light when unexpectedly, Shundra received a call from the guy's wife.

"Hello, my name is Annie. Your number is in my husband's cell phone. May I ask who is this? she said.

"My name is Shundra. Who is your husband?" Shundra replied.

Shundra was not surprised at the name she gave; neither was she impressed with his cheating ass, so she apologized to Annie and promised to end whatever he thought was going to happen between the two of them. And it was over. Instantly, Shundra deleted his number from her phone and obliterated him for life. *Jerk,* she thought.

Life experiences taught Shundra many things to elude while moving forward in relationships: communication, resolving conflict, and cheating were a few of the obvious red flags. However, she was ambivalent when it came to mimicking her lover's parents' awe-inspiring relationship while neglecting to create remarkable memories of her own to reminisce. Her lover needed to understand he was not his father, and she was not his mother. What worked for his parents may not necessarily work for them. She came to realize such a situation was damaging to the relationship when issues with communication and resolving conflict existed as well.

Knowing the love languages of a potential mate is a prerequisite for successful relationships, so meeting Edmond was just the beginning of maybe a long journey of learning and understanding his short- and long-term intentional involvement with Shundra. It took many dates and discussions outside of DEC to determine the right criteria for choosing Edmond as Shundra's mate.

Shundra spent several fascinating months dancing with Edmond before he showed other interests: late-night dinners during the week, late evenings of spontaneous adventures, road trips, bowling, skating, movies, plays, musicals, hiking, and picnics, to name a few.

It was also comforting knowing Anthony no longer intimidated her with persistent stares and his refusal to speak whenever he saw Edmond with her. Edmond was now claiming his territory, and Shundra had no objections to him being around to protect her.

So far, everything was going well in their relationship, but Shundra needed to probe further to determine their compatibility of life's vision, purpose, and beliefs.

One cozy and romantic evenings at the park, Shundra said to Edmond, "I enjoy the time we spend together. I think our relationship is moving to a higher level. What are your thoughts, and how do you feel about me?

"Wow! My baby doesn't beat around the bush, Edmond said while listening attentively. 'And, I like it,' he added before replying to the question.

Shundra corrected him immediately, "It's called effective

114

communication; no need to waste words or valuable time. *She wasn't kidding with her line of questioning. If Edmond didn't meet her criteria, she wasn't spending any more of her precious time in a relationship going nowhere.*

"Well, said Edmond, to answer your question, yes, I feel you are the one—the girl I want in my life always.

"Seriously, what does that mean? Shundra asked.

"It means I am in this relationship for the long haul. I don't want a playmate; I'm looking for a wife.

Shundra smiled. *Hum! Understands and goes straight to the point—communication checked!*

The interrogation continued. "Are you a Christian? she asked.

"Yes, I am, he replied.

"What type of relationship do you have with God?

"Well, I have an intimate and personal relationship with God. I walk in his presence every day, living and trusting, and abiding by his word. He is my strength when I need him, and trust me; I need him a lot! he confirmed. 'God provides my purpose for living.'

By the expression on Shundra's face, Edmond wasn't sure if she was amazed or mystified. "Tell me, Shundra, do I meet your criteria? Or am I boring you with my lifestyle?

"No, you are not boring me at all. I'm enjoying our conversation. But, not so fast, Shundra said. Are you sure you can provide my needs and my wants? I'm looking for genuine love—someone who does what's in my best interest and stands by his convictions.

"Shundra, he said, you are amazing. I love your intellect and the fact that you know what you want in a man.

"Edmond, she replied, I like that I can be myself without you thinking my openness and honesty is malicious. I appreciate that privilege so much, and I enjoy talking with you.

"Same here, baby, he responded. And, this is why I will go over and beyond, with God's help, to make you happy, to get the things you need and want.

"Does this include counseling, if needed? Shundra asked with a big smile on her face.

"Whatever it takes, baby. I told you I am in this relationship for the long haul, hoping marriage is in our future, he said.

"That's a good thing, Shundra replied. I know our relationship is relatively new, and we've had no disagreements or arguments so far, but every relationship has them from time to time. What is your idea of handling conflict resolutions? she asked.

"That's a hard question to answer because I am still learning your love languages, he replied.

No, this man did not mention LOVE LANGUAGES! If he understands Love Languages, we've won half of our battles already. Thank you, Lord!

"For now, he said, I can promise you this—we are not sleeping in separate beds; we are not playing the no-speaking game, and we are not closing our eyes before a kiss, and the assurance that we still love one another. Relationships take effort and the willingness to put in the hard work, and I am ready to do it all. We will close our eyes knowing this too shall pass, and we will find a resolution that works best for both of us.

Wow! Is this man for real or not? He is very intriguing! Resolving Conflicts—checked, till proven otherwise!

"Sounds like you had a great role model in making relationships work, Shundra said with approval in her voice.

"My parents, who are deceased now, were married for over 50 years. I watched them through ups and downs, while still showing nothing but love and respect for one another. They taught me all things are possible with God; therefore, divorce was not an option for them. Although I am not my father and you are not my mom, I stand on their convictions in working through struggles, because I believe in God, as they did, said Edmond.

Checkmate! Shundra grins inwardly, trying not to show how sweet it is—those famous words, "I am not my father, and you are not my mom."

"So, you don't cheat, at all? Shundra asked.

"You remind me of my mom with your 50-plus questions, your honesty, and your openness, Shundra. No, baby, what we have feels right, and I believe you are the one. I do not and will not cheat. I'd rather leave if it comes to that. Any other questions? he asked.

"No, she responded. Let's enjoy the rest of the evening before the sun goes down.

Edmond nodded his head with gratitude, kissed her forehead, and responded, "My thoughts, exactly! Whew!"

25

The Moment She Waited For

Shundra went to work feeling relaxed and completed the project her manager was expecting before lunch. *What a productive day*, she thought, impressed with her accomplishments on the job. *Now, it's time to concentrate on the character of Kenneth's true nature. Where should I start?* she wondered.

<u>Monday - Lunch at 2:45 p.m.</u>

After the prom, Kenneth called and thanked Shundra for the invite. He said he had a gratifying experience, and Shundra was thrilled.

"What are your plans now that you are graduating? Kenneth asked.

"Well, according to my mom, I only have two choices: GO TO COLLEGE or GET A JOB! And, that means the first day after graduation! she replied bashfully. And since I haven't applied to any colleges, I guess a job it is!

Kenneth was eager to assist Shundra. "Well, maybe I can help you with that. A friend of mine works for a commercial architect company that is looking for an architectural designer assistant to schedule reviews and evaluation meetings with their clients. I will call him and see if he can get you an interview.

"Yes, that would be awesome! Thank you, Kenneth, Shundra said excitedly.

"Anything for my girl! he replied. Let's celebrate your graduation early tonight," he suggested. And, Shundra happily obliged.

Reb Lobster was their first stop; not quite the romantic gesture as the Michelangelo Italian Restaurant. After dinner, they went to his friend's birthday party. Of course, they didn't stay too long because Kenneth had other plans for the night on his mind.

He pulled into the apartment complex, where he and Jason shared a two-bedroom apartment. Inside, you could see the living room and the kitchen as you walked through the front door. The bedrooms were adjacent from the living area: Kenneth's room on the right and Jason's room on the left.

After showing Shundra around the place, Kenneth turned on some music and offered her a mixed drink. Her demeanor sluggishly changed, and Kenneth knew it was time to make his move. Her eyes turned bright, and her words began to slur.

"Baby, I think you are tipsy, he said, grinning as if his intentions were innocent. 'Come on, let's go to my room,' he said.

Shundra agreed that she was tipsy and willing followed him to his room.

They laid across the bed, and Kenneth proceeded, like before, without hesitation, to kiss her, starting with her neck, earlobes, and finally her lips while slowly removing her clothes. He maneuvered his way to her boobs, gently massaging her nipples with his tongue, before reaching the secretion of her body. "Baby, you taste sweet," Kenneth moaned.

He looked upward to see her facial expression: eyes closed,

mouth slightly opened, seemingly attempting to speak, but then, the moment Shundra was waiting for, happened—Kenneth gently inserted himself inside her, and it felt painfully good!

In and out, slowly and faster, he moved inside her, careful not to break his rhythm. Then, ten minutes later, they climaxed, letting out loud groans of satisfaction. And it was over.

Their sweaty bodies laid close together, motionless for 40 minutes before it was time for Shundra to shower, get dressed, and go home. While she was dressing, Kenneth was smiling and staring immensely.

"The afterglow looks beautiful on you, he said.

"Afterglow? Shundra asked.

"Sexual satisfaction, baby!

"Shut up, Kenneth, she responded.

"Why? Didn't you enjoy it too? he asked, grinning like he was the man!

"Yes, I did, she said, trying not to reveal too much excitement.

"Do you want more of me, baby? he asked in his sexy voice, feeling confident of her response.

Shundra smiled and said, "Of course, after I recover from all the soreness.

"All right, baby, he said, smiling. I'll take you home."

Yeah, baby! I'm the man! Shundra ain't had nothing like this before, he thought to himself.

26

The Calm Before the Storm

Shundra had no idea there was a witching hour hanging over her and Kenneth's relationship. The cool breezes and sunshine ended, just when she thought her love life and her one year on the job as an architectural designer were great. Working from 8 to 5 left little time to spend with Kenneth during the week, and weekends were debatable since his job required him to work some weekends, so he said. The lack of quality time put a damper on their relationship, and Shundra didn't realize it until it was too late.

Their sex life, in Shundra's opinion, was terrific but was scarce these days, and so her insecurities started to kick in. Kenneth didn't seem to mind that their sex life was drastically changing. He said he understood that Shundra was a hardworking woman and not always available. What he didn't say was that if she weren't available, someone else would be.

Her intuition was getting stronger by the day, and she knew she had to satisfy this craving before she went insane. "Kenneth, are we okay? Should I be worried about our relationship? she asked him.

Of course, his response was, "No, babe, we're good. You love me, right?

"You know I love you, Kenneth.

"Then, you have nothing to worry about. I love you too," he said.

But, his response did not satisfy Shundra's craving. Instead, her intuition grew even stronger. She needed to prove to herself that she was right. *He's lying, and I know it. I guess I have to catch him in the act!* Shundra thought.

Kenneth wasn't a light sleeper, so when he fell asleep, Shundra took his keys from the dresser, went to Ace Hardware store and made a key to his apartment. Then, she gently placed the keys back on the dresser and crawled between the sheets, snuggling as close as she could to his warm body. *Game on! I will catch you*! she thought before she closed her eyes.

The following weekend, Shundra left work early. She called Kenneth to let him know she was coming over, but he didn't answer the phone. Instead of leaving him a message, she decided she would stalk his apartment to see who was coming and going while she was busy being "a hardworking woman." After two hours of seeing nothing, she called him again. Still, he didn't answer, so she used her key.

Shundra walked into the surprise of her life: there Kenneth was screwing some woman, who was moaning and groaning and calling him "Papi." He didn't hear Shundra when she entered his room because the music was so loud. Seeing Shundra standing there surprised him and his lady friend too!

Shundra was devastated. She ran out of the apartment to her car and drove off in an intense rage. Kenneth called out to her, but he wasn't able to run after her. He was naked, and his friend was screaming and demanding an explanation as well.

When Shundra finally calmed down enough to stop for gas, she saw a guy who lived in her neighborhood. She didn't know him well, but he'd made it known he was interested in her many times before. When he saw her, he quickly came over and offered to pump her gas. He also mentioned that she should stop by his garage sometime, since she lived so close by, adding that he lived in the house in the back of the shop. Never before was Shundra interest in this man, but tonight, she didn't care. She wanted to get even with Kenneth, so she asked the guy, "What are you doing tonight? He wasn't expecting that sort of response!

"Nothing, he said. Would you like to come by tonight? he asked.

"Why not, said Shundra. Tonight is a good night.

"Okay, the guy said. Follow me."

Shundra did just that. It wasn't long before she was in bed with him, moaning, groaning, and intentionally calling him "Papi" as if Kenneth could see or hear her.

Every day for the next two weeks, Kenneth called, but Shundra did not answer his calls. Fifteen days later, she experienced abdominal pains like severe cramps on her lower right side and burning when she urinated. She finally made an appointment to see a doctor and discovered she had all the symptoms of gonorrhea: consequences of her promiscuous behavior. The doctor injected her with ceftriaxone (250 mg) used for severe infections of the urinary tract. He also gave her oral azithromycin (1g) for sexually transmitted diseases. He said the symptoms should be gone a few days after receiving the treatment.

This wasn't the first encounter Shundra had had with guys she didn't know well, but it was the first time she experienced an STD, and she wasn't too fond of it. *Who would be?* Before, it was all about having a good time, and she insisted on using a condom. But this time was different: a heart filled with emotions and revenge. The one time she neglected to mention a condom caused her much suffering and self-pity.

Kenneth tried to apologize for his behavior. He promised never to cheat again, but Shundra didn't want to hear it. "Kenneth, you hurt me, and I don't know if I can forgive you, she said.

"I know. And I am so sorry. It just happened. She came by, and before I realized what was about to happen, it happened. I didn't mean to hurt you, said Kenneth.

"I don't believe that. I do think you are sorry that you got caught. But, I don't trust you anymore, said Shundra. I think we should go our separate ways.

"Please forgive me, baby. I promise that nothing like this will happen ever again, he said.

But Shundra said, "No, I don't want to be in a relationship with someone I don't trust."

The two of them were in a terrible predicament. Shundra wasn't willing to forgive Kenneth, and Kenneth didn't know he needed to forgive Shundra. Two wrongs didn't make their situation right, and because Shundra couldn't forgive herself, she couldn't forgive Kenneth either. He could only hope that in time; maybe he could win her heart again, so he vowed never to stop trying to win her back.

27

The Man of Her Prayers

The doorbell rings and Shundra peeked out the window before she answered the door. A 2019 silver Audi was sitting in her driveway with petals of yellow roses with red tips trailing from the passenger side of the car to the front door. She could hardly contain the butterflies swarming inside her. "Just a minute," she said. 'Coming!' she yelled after freshening up her candy-red lipstick. Then, with her sparkling eyes and charming smile, she greeted him at the door, "Hey, delicious.

"Hey, gorgeous, Edmond replied while bending down to place a gentle kiss on those candy-red lips.

"What's behind your back? Shundra asked.

"Darn, girl! Can you wait till I present the gift?

"No, I can't, she replied while wrapping her arms around his waist, trying to reach the gift.

He turned from side to side to keep her from seeing what was behind his back. "Are you ready to go? he asked.

She looked down to put the key in her purse, then she looked up, and the roses were staring her in the face; the aroma was incredible.

"Aww, thank you, babe, she said. 'They are beautiful!'

He grabbed her hand and walked her to the car. He opened the car door, and lying on the seat was a small velvet box. Shundra reached for the box. *Is this what I think it is?*

When she turned around, Edmond was on one knee, proposing. He took the box, opened it, and said, "I am the man of your present, your past, and your future. Marry me, and I promise to spend the rest of my life protecting you, learning your love languages, and making you happy. Whatever obstacles come our way, we will face them together without failure, because we devoted our life to God, and he will uphold the marriage, as he created it to be. You are the one. Marry me, babe!

Tears ran from Shundra's eyes. Instead of her leaping for joy and saying "Yes, I will marry you," she responded, "But, what if—

Before she could complete her statement, Edmond stood up, embraced her, and said, "Baby, there's no what-ifs. Communication is the key. The Bible says, 'Love is patient, love is kind. It does not envy, it does not boast, it is not proud.' (1 Cor. 13: 4, New International Version, n.d.). God is the Creator of marriage. Consulting him together; every step of the way is where we will begin. You are the one. Marry me, babe.

"Edmond, she said with the taste of tears running from her eyes to her mouth, I can feel how much you love God. You position yourself under him, seeking how he wants every situation handled.

To me, that means you are responsible, accountable, and because of that, I will follow you anywhere, always! Yes! Yes! Yes! I will marry you! Shundra said.

She continued to speak, "Baby, your name, Edmond, means 'prosperous and protector,' and you are all that and more to me. I love you! Yes, I will marry you!"

And, after she said those precious words, Edmond slipped the ring on her finger. Then, he kissed her with delight and whispered, "Your name means you are spiritually intense and can sting or charm, and I can handle both. Your name brings love and new beginnings. It also attracts money, he laughed. We are off to a good start already. I'm hungry, babe. Let's go eat!"

28

One Year and Two Days Later

The crowd stood as Shundra slowly walked down the aisle. She looked elegant with her hourglass shape covered beautifully in a floor-length, sleeveless, jewel-neckline gown with a see-through back covered in pearls. She's glowing and feeling like the happiest person on earth, while Edmond eagerly awaits to recite his vows to his wife-to-be.

The officiant, Pastor Goodman, with St. Luke Church, announced the exchange of the wedding vows. "The bride and groom have prepared their sacred promises to each other. It is their words, their intentions, and their vision that must define and shape this marriage."

"Edmond, you may present your vows," he said.

"Shundra, I promise, said Edmond, life will not push us apart. I will learn and execute your love languages. When I see things are going in the wrong direction, I will lead us to God's counsel so we can pray together and stay together. I will meet your expectations and pray that you meet mine. *Everyone laughs*. Learning one another will be our priority, said Edmond. I am willing to put in the required time and more to get us to this point. I will never stop responding to your needs, so you never have a reason to stop responding to mine. *Everyone laughs again.* I will provide beyond my mental capacity, depending on my faith in God, to provide where I cannot. I will love, honor, and respect you for the rest of our days together. These things, I promise, as God is my witness. I love you, baby."

Pastor Goodman said, "Let the church say amen!" And, Edmond sealed his promises with the ring.

"Shundra, you may now present your vows," said Pastor Goodman.

"Wow! Shundra said, barely holding back the tears of joy. Honey, I agree with all you said, one hundred percent. *Everyone laughs.* I promise to follow your guidance under God. I will honor you as my husband and build the house we share into a home. I will be loyal to you all the days of my life. I will pray for you, pray with you, and pray for us. I will praise God for you, the man he has given to me, to be my husband. I will love you during the storms of life and peace after that. These things I promise, as God is my witness. I love you too, baby."

"Amen, amen!" said Pastor Goodman. Then, Shundra sealed her promises with the ring.

"I now pronounce you husband and wife, said Pastor Goodman. Edmond, you may kiss your bride."

Passionately, Edmond kisses his bride, tongue and all, as if they were the only two people in the room. Gayle yelled from the audience, "Save some for the honeymoon!" The crowd laughed out loud while clapping in agreement, as Mr. and Mrs. Johnston stood there smitten.

Finally, the spell broke, and the couple turned toward the crowd, walked hand in hand, smiling from ear to ear, and ducking from the heart-shaped confetti tossed upon them.

They were married now and couldn't wait to consummate

the marriage. During the reception, Shundra whispered to Edmond, "Can we go now? Her eyes were sparkling, and Edmond knew why.

Without hesitation, he said, "Let's go!" so they sneaked out the side door without anyone noticing and headed to their hotel room for the night.

The foreplay began as Edmond kissed her forehead, her nose, her lips, and her earlobes. Gently, his lips moved towards her neck, her breasts, her stomach, and down her thighs and inner legs, exploring every part of her body, using all five senses to generate pleasure. He turned her over and rubbed her body in oil, then entered inside her from behind. Shundra moaned with gratification. He turned her on her back and blissfully inserted himself in and out until that moment of anticipation: the first orgasm as husband and wife, and Shundra's legs shake, relaxed and fulfilled.

Edmond fell asleep quickly, and there was no doubt in Shundra's mind that he was highly satisfied. Before closing her eyes, she looked up and silently thanked God for blessing her with the man of her dreams. *The brokenness and pieces of my life have finally come together. For this, Lord, I thank you!*

And then, she prayed out loud, "Tonight marks the beginning of our lives. Father, I pray that you be with us and keep us from harm and separation for the rest of our days together. Amen!"

Then, she fell asleep, expecting nothing but sweet dreams.

www.ingramcontent.com/pod-product-compliance
Lightning Source LLC
Chambersburg PA
CBHW060125260626
47160CB00005B/2019